"You comforted him. The way you've
been comforting me tonight. Thank
you."

But saying the words wasn't enough to express
her gratitude for what the sheriff had done for
her son. She rose up on tiptoe and pressed her
lips to his.

"Jessie…" Chance's voice, and his deep blue eyes,
held a warning. But before she could heed it and
step back, his arms slid around her and pulled
her closer. He clutched her against the hard
muscles of his chest. Then he lowered his head
and he kissed her back.

He really kissed her, like she'd been longing
for him to kiss her. His lips moved against hers
with all the desire that she'd tried denying she
felt for him. But watching him these past couple
of weeks with Tommy, seeing his patience and
kindness, she was afraid that she'd gone beyond
just wanting him.

Dear Reader,

I hope you enjoy reading *Single Dad Sheriff* as much as I enjoyed writing it. This story is one of my favorites thanks to an eight-year-old matchmaker named Tommy Phillips. Tommy is such a smart and precocious kid. He's wise far beyond his years and wiser than some of the stubborn adults in his life. He reminds me a bit of my youngest, who's so smart that I struggle to keep up with her. His similarity to my daughter is no doubt why he has become one of my favorite characters.

Just like my daughter, Tommy is very logical, has great perspective and is also very determined. He's determined to have the family he's always wanted, and he'll work very hard to get two stubborn single parents together. I hope Tommy's matchmaking touches your heart like it has mine.

Happy reading!

Lisa Childs

Single Dad Sheriff

LISA CHILDS

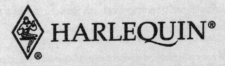

HARLEQUIN®

TORONTO • NEW YORK • LONDON
AMSTERDAM • PARIS • SYDNEY • HAMBURG
STOCKHOLM • ATHENS • TOKYO • MILAN • MADRID
PRAGUE • WARSAW • BUDAPEST • AUCKLAND

Recycling programs
for this product may
not exist in your area.

ISBN-13: 978-0-373-75328-4

SINGLE DAD SHERIFF

Copyright © 2010 by Lisa Childs-Theeuwes.

This edition published by arrangement with Harlequin Books S.A.

For questions and comments about the quality of this book
please contact us at Customer_eCare@Harlequin.ca

® and TM are trademarks of the publisher. Trademarks indicated with
® are registered in the United States Patent and Trademark Office, the
Canadian Trade Marks Office and in other countries.

www.eHarlequin.com

Printed in U.S.A.

ABOUT THE AUTHOR

Bestselling, award-winning author Lisa Childs writes paranormal and contemporary romance for Harlequin and Silhouette Books. She lives on thirty acres in west Michigan with her husband, two daughters, a talkative Siamese and a long-haired Chihuahua who thinks she's a Rottweiler. Lisa loves hearing from readers, who can contact her through her Web site, www.lisachilds.com, or snail mail address, P.O. Box 139, Marne, MI 49435.

Books by Lisa Childs

HARLEQUIN AMERICAN ROMANCE

1198—UNEXPECTED BRIDE*
1210—THE BEST MAN'S BRIDE*
1222—FOREVER HIS BRIDE*
1230—FINALLY A BRIDE*
1245—ONCE A LAWMAN†
1258—ONCE A HERO†
1274—ONCE A COP†
1301—HIS BABY SURPRISE

HARLEQUIN NEXT

TAKING BACK MARY ELLEN BLACK
LEARNING TO HULA
CHRISTMAS PRESENCE
  "Secret Santa"

HARLEQUIN INTRIGUE

 664—RETURN OF THE LAWMAN
 720—SARAH'S SECRETS
 758—BRIDAL RECONNAISSANCE
 834—THE SUBSTITUTE SISTER
1213—MYSTERY LOVER

*The Wedding Party
†Citizen's Police Academy

For my daughters, Ashley and Chloe,
who make me so proud to be their mother!

Chapter One

"Sheriff, I wanna report something missing," the boy said, his blue eyes earnest as he stared across the desk.

Chance glanced up at his gray-haired secretary, who leaned against the doorjamb of his dark-paneled office. A smile curved her lips, and her eyes twinkled with amusement. He winked at her before returning his focus to the complainant in front of him. From his small size and the gaps in his teeth, the redheaded, freckle-faced boy was probably about seven or eight. Chance doubted the kid had anything more important than a library book or a bike missing, and unless Forest Glen was having an unprecedented crime wave, that item had been misplaced rather than stolen.

Since he had nothing else to do besides make another expensive, frustrating call to his lawyer, Chance pulled out a form to humor the boy. He'd brought Forest Glen police department into the twenty-first century when he'd been hired a couple of months ago, and a computer sat on his clutter-free desk. But he wasn't about to open an official investigation until he knew more about the boy's complaint.

"I'd be happy to take your report. What's your name,

son?" He coughed, nearly choking on that last word since he could so rarely use it to address his own child. He needed to call his lawyer again.

"My name is Tommy Phillips," the boy replied.

If Chance really intended to open a case file for the kid, he would have asked him for more information, like his address and date of birth. Instead he cut to the chase. "So what have you lost, Tommy Phillips?"

"My dad."

Chance's breath left his lungs in a gasp that echoed Eleanor's. The older woman stepped forward and put her hand on the boy's shoulder. "Did your father pass away, honey?"

Tommy shook his head. "No." But then his smooth brow furrowed and he shrugged. "I don't know. Maybe."

"You don't know where your father is?" Chance asked.

"No, Sheriff, he's missing," Tommy said, his voice rising slightly with impatience, as if he were annoyed that Chance wasn't following. "Can you *please* find him for me?"

Setting aside the pen and the form, Chance pushed back his chair and came around the desk. He crouched in front of the boy and asked, "How long has your father been gone, Tommy?"

The kid's gaze slid away until he stared down at the hole in the knee of his jeans. He plucked at the loose threads with fingers that trembled. "Since before I was born."

Ohh...

"I think we better talk to your mother, Tommy."

Chance straightened to his full six feet and pushed a hand through his dark hair.

"Why? She won't tell you anything about my dad." Tommy's face flushed with color that nearly connected the dots of his freckles. "I don't even know who he is."

"Yeah, we definitely need to talk to your mom." Chance turned toward Eleanor. "Is she waiting out front?"

"No, he came in all by himself."

"You did?" Chance asked the boy. He'd moved to Forest Glen, Michigan, because it was the kind of town where kids could play outside without worrying about stray bullets from a drive-by shooting or drug dealers harassing them—both things Chance had dealt with as a detective in Chicago. Still, it surprised him that a child this young was out all alone.

Tommy nodded. "I rode my bike."

"And your mom doesn't know you're here?"

"No."

Chance swallowed a sigh. "Tommy, you can't take off without telling your mom where you're going."

"She doesn't even know I'm gone," the boy assured him. "If she knew I was here, she'd freak out. She won't help me find my dad. But you have to."

"I do?"

The redhead bobbed in a vigorous nod. "You have to 'cause it's your job. If somebody's missing, you gotta find 'em."

"Tommy, this situation is a little different from a usual missing person's case. Your dad didn't just disappear." But Chance wasn't the one who owed the boy an explanation. "You really need to talk to your mom."

The kid snorted his disgust. "Weren't you listening?"

Eleanor choked, covering a laugh with a cough.

"I told you, she won't say anything about my dad," precocious Tommy reminded him.

"But that's not a matter for the sheriff's office, son."

The kid sprang out of the chair. "I thought you were supposed to help people!" Tears glittered in his blue eyes, but he blinked them back and shoved past Chance. Probably anxious to get away before he broke down and cried.

Chance caught the back of the boy's hooded sweatshirt. "Hold up. I didn't say that I wouldn't help you."

Tommy turned toward him. One tear streaked down his face. "You will? You'll help me find my dad?"

The kid wasn't playing him with those tears; it really meant that much to him to find out who his dad was. And maybe it was because Chance couldn't dry his own son's tears that he found himself gently wiping away Tommy's with his thumb. "Sure, I'll help you."

The boy threw his arms around Chance's waist in a hug of gratitude and joy. "Thank you! Thank you, Sheriff!"

Chance patted the redhead and then lifted his gaze to Eleanor's. The older woman's lips pulled down in a frown of disapproval.

Yeah, he had no business getting involved in something that was clearly family business. But despite Tommy being a couple years younger than Matthew, he reminded Chance of his own son and how much he wished someone could help reunite them.

"CAN YOU HELP ME find him?" Jessie Phillips asked, panic pressing on her chest.

"Sure, Jess," Bruce Johnson replied. "Christopher and I will ride into town and look for him. He probably went down to the ice cream parlor."

"He was only supposed to come over *here*." Her knees shook with anxiety as she leaned on the gate of her neighbor's white fence. She'd walked to the house four down from hers to call Tommy home for dinner, only to find out that he had never showed up to play with his friend.

"Didn't you see him at all?" she asked, desperate to know if they'd at least caught a glimpse of her missing child.

Christopher shook his head, tumbling a light brown curl across his forehead and over the top of the wire rims of his glasses. "No, Ms. Phillips, he never showed up."

"Don't worry," Bruce said with a reassuring smile. "We'll track him down for you and send him right home." The guy, thin and slightly built like his son, slid an arm around Christopher's shoulders. "We'll finish our game later."

Christopher, probably picking up on the concern that the adults weren't quite able to hide, dropped his beloved birthday-gift glove and rushed past Jessie out the gate to the driveway where his mom's minivan was parked. Then he turned and called back, "Hey, Ms. Phillips, there's a cop car by your house."

Jessie's heart skipped a beat. "Cop car?"

Forest Glen had only one: the new sheriff's white sedan with the light bar on the roof. The two deputies used their own vehicles. One had an extended cab pickup truck and the other an old Jeep, and they had only a light that snapped onto the dash inside. It was the sheriff's sedan parked at the curb outside her house. The lights weren't flashing. Was that a good sign or a bad one?

Her legs shook even more as she ran down the sidewalk. "Tommy! Tommy!"

"Hey, Mom," he called back from where he stood on the front porch. A man's big hand cupped her son's shoulder, as if he were keeping the little boy from running off.

What trouble had Tommy gotten into?

She didn't care. At the moment, all that mattered was that he was all right. She stumbled up the steps of the small Craftsman bungalow. Then she dropped to her knees and threw her arms around Tommy's slight body.

"You scared me half to death," she admonished him, her shaky voice weakening the reprimand. "When I went down to the Johnsons' to get you for dinner and they said you'd never showed up..." Tears threatened again. She'd fought them off earlier because she'd needed to keep her wits about her to find her son. But now that he was safe, she could shed tears of relief.

"I guess he was wrong," a deep voice murmured.

She glanced up at the sheriff, her confusion increasing because the man himself was such a distraction. His eyes were nearly as deep a blue as his uniform, and his hair was dark. Even though it was short, it looked thick enough for her to lose her fingers in it. She blinked, trying to clear that image from her mind.

"What was he wrong about?" she asked. And how much trouble had it gotten him into?

"He told me that you wouldn't even notice him gone."

She sucked in a breath and pulled back from her son. Then she cupped his little pointed chin in her palm and lifted it, so he had to meet her gaze. His face flushed nearly the same shade of burnt orange as his freckles. He wriggled free of her loose hold and stared down at his feet. "Why would you say something like that, Tommy?" How could he think that when she told him so often how much she loved him? "Of course I'd notice if you were gone."

He scuffed the toe of his tennis shoe against the stained boards of the porch floor. "I know, Mom."

"Then why would you tell Sheriff Drayton that I wouldn't?"

His thin shoulders lifted in a slight shrug. "I dunno…"

Since her son wasn't forthcoming, she turned toward the sheriff for answers. Her gaze locked with his intense one, and she nearly forgot her question as her pulse quickened. She had never let a man's looks, however handsome, distract her, though.

Forcing her focus back to what mattered most to her, she explained, "I—I thought he was at the neighbor's. He's only allowed to ride his bike down the sidewalk the four houses to theirs." She gestured back down the block to the Johnsons' brick Cape Cod with the white fence. "I…I don't understand why he's with you. Why are you bringing Tommy home? Did he get in some kind of trouble? Where did you find him?"

"In my office," the sheriff replied.

"Did someone bring him in to you?" Had her child

been out wandering the streets of Forest Glen? Not that there were many streets for him to wander, but still…

"I rode my bike, Mom," Tommy replied in a long-suffering tone. "And I didn't get run over crossing any streets."

She swallowed a gasp of fear at the image of him out there, alone, in traffic—not that there was a whole lot of that in Forest Glen, either. But if he'd crossed paths with the mayor's mother in her pink Cadillac…

She shuddered at the thought of what could have happened to her son. The eight-year-old was too independent for his own good and hers. "That's not the point."

"You always say I can't cross streets, but I know how to look both ways first. I'm not stupid."

No. That he wasn't. "You know you were only supposed to go over to play with Christopher. Why did you go to the sheriff's office?"

Her son pressed his lips together in a stubborn gesture that Jessie knew a little too well. She forced aside some of her joy in his coming safely home to admonish him, "Tommy—"

But he pushed open the front door and ran inside, slamming the door behind him.

"Tommy!" Heat rushed to her face with embarrassment that the sheriff had witnessed her son's disrespect. Even though his hair wasn't quite as bright as hers, Tommy had more of the notorious redhead temper than she did. "I'm sorry. Really, he has better manners than that. I don't know what's the matter with him."

"I do," Chance Drayton replied.

She remembered his name from the town council meeting where they'd voted to hire the ex-Marine who'd just returned from his second tour of duty in

Afghanistan. A reservist, he'd left behind a career as a detective in Chicago to serve his country. But until the next public election, he was just an interim sheriff since the town's old one—old as in former and really elderly—had just retired.

She doubted the big city detective would put his name on the ballot. He was probably already bored out of his mind in Forest Glen, considering where he'd worked and lived before. He wouldn't be sticking around. But Jessie had mentioned the town meeting and the man to her son, and ever since, Tommy had wanted to meet the Marine.

She rubbed at the tension headache forming between her brows. "He told you? But he won't tell his mother..."

"He said you won't talk about it."

Dread clenched her stomach as realization dawned. "Oh..."

"Yeah." The sheriff nodded. "He came into my office to file a missing person's report."

She sucked in a breath. She didn't need to ask because she already knew whom Tommy had reported missing. But all she managed to utter was another, "Oh..."

"He wants me to find his father for him."

She moved her hand to her throat, where her pulse pounded as rapidly as it had when she'd discovered Tommy had never gone to the Johnsons'. "I'm sorry he asked you to do that. He doesn't understand..."

"Like he said, he's not stupid. He actually seems to be a pretty intelligent kid. I'm sure he'd understand if you explained."

A twinge of guilt struck, causing Jessie to wince. She couldn't tell Tommy the truth without risking her son hating her. She doubted that the former Marine would condone her cowardice.

"This is a family matter," she pointed out, her shoulders tensing with defensiveness, "and he shouldn't have bothered you with it."

"He was no bother," he assured her.

"I'm glad, and I'm grateful that you brought him home," she said. "But I'm sure you're very busy. I wouldn't want to keep you from anything."

"Busy?" His deep blue eyes glinted with humor. "The only thing Tommy kept me from was finding Mrs. Wilson's cat."

"Which one?" The elderly widow had so many that Jessie was surprised she would have noticed one missing.

He shrugged. "She didn't say when she called it in."

"Those cats are like her kids, so I'm sure she's concerned. I better not keep you from her. Thanks again for bringing my son home." She turned toward the door Tommy had slammed behind him. She needed to have a talk with her son about his behavior—not his father.

She'd been avoiding that last conversation for eight years. Until recently, Tommy had been fine with having no father. He'd only occasionally asked about his dad, but when Jessie had replied that he didn't have one, he hadn't pressed for more information. Then.

"Wait," the sheriff said. "I have a question for you."

She closed her eyes and drew in a breath before turning back to him. Heat rushed to her face as she wondered exactly what else Tommy had told him, besides the fact his mother wouldn't notice him missing, and what Chance Drayton must think of her because of it. But she had stopped caring what people thought of her years ago, when she'd decided to become a single mother. "Yes?"

"Where do you want me to put his bike?" he asked. "I have it in the trunk of my car."

She expelled that breath in a soft sigh. "I should probably have you keep it there—after what he did. I can't believe he rode all the way to your office." She shuddered. "Alone."

Thank goodness he'd been wearing a sweatshirt or he might have gotten cold despite spring coming early to western Michigan this year. March was definitely going out like a lamb after having come in with a heck of a snowstorm a few weeks ago. But the recent warm temperatures had melted all the snow and revived the dead grass.

Without a word, the sheriff walked down the steps to the car parked at her curb. She followed him and remarked, "This is where, as sheriff, you're supposed to reassure me that it was only a few blocks and Forest Glen is a safe town."

He touched a button on his key chain and the trunk opened with a pop and metal clink. A shotgun and extra ammo were strapped under the lid. Tommy's small black bike, with its wide tires and handle bar grips, lay atop a first aid kit, a hazmat suit, road flares and a roll of yellow crime scene tape. "As sheriff, I'd be a fool to assure you that any place is truly safe."

A slight shiver raced across her skin along with the breeze that had begun to cool as night approached. Tommy should have been home over an hour ago. "I know. That's why I only allow him to go as far as the Johnsons' by himself. And I usually stand on the porch and watch to make sure he gets there. But the phone was ringing as he rode off. I thought he stopped at their gate…"

"He didn't," Sheriff Drayton said, his deep voice betraying a hint of the disapproval she already thought she'd glimpsed in his eyes.

She didn't care if he disapproved of her; she didn't care what he thought. Yet she replied, "I'll talk to him about disobeying me."

Muscles rippled in his broad back as he leaned over and lifted out the bike. Holding it in one hand, he slammed the trunk lid closed with the other. Jessie reached for the bike, but he stepped around her and carried it up the steps to the porch.

"Thank you," she said.

He arched a dark brow as if questioning her gratitude. "I thought you weren't sure you wanted his bike back."

"I'm not sure about the bike," she admitted, "but thanks again for bringing my son back." With a smile, she added, "I'd hoped he would never get driven home in a police car, but I figured that if he ever did, he'd at least be older than eight."

"He wasn't riding in the back," he replied with a reassuring smile.

And Jessie's pulse quickened in reaction to the sparkle in his blue eyes and the curve of his lips.

"He was sitting there for a little while, though. He had to check out where the criminals ride, you know." The sheriff's smile widened even more.

"I'm sure he went over every inch of the car and asked you a million questions."

"He's an inquisitive kid."

"I know," Jessie said with a weary sigh. And now he didn't accept her answer about his father. He wanted more information, information she wasn't sure he was ready to learn or that she was ready to tell him.

"Did you know that he wants to find his dad so badly he'd file a missing person's report on him?"

"I didn't think he'd actually file a report," she said. But ever since the Johnsons had moved to Forest Glen, Tommy had been envious of Christopher and Bruce's loving father-son relationship. Over the past year, he'd begun to ask more questions about his own dad. "Of course, it's not a real report. You wouldn't take one from an eight-year-old."

"Kids should feel they can report things to the police," he said.

She nodded her agreement. "Abuse. Crimes. But nothing like that is going on here. Your protection isn't necessary."

"Probably not."

"Probably?" Her temper sparked. "You better not be implying that I'm abusing my child!"

"Not physically," he said. "He told me he's never been to the doctor or hospital for anything more serious than an earache and his shots."

"You interrogated my son?" Her anger ran hot now as she realized what he'd done.

His voice deepened with impatience and a trace of defensiveness. "It's my job."

"To grill an eight-year-old?"

"To find out why he asked for my help."

"He doesn't need your help," she insisted. She would answer Tommy's questions when he was older, like when he was about to leave for college. But she couldn't tell him now because she didn't want to risk losing him.

"I promised I'd give it to him," he said.

"You promised what exactly?" she asked as dread, almost as intense as when she'd discovered Tommy missing, wound through her.

"I promised that I'd help him find his father."

Chapter Two

"You shouldn't have done that!" the redhead exclaimed, her creamy skin paling even more with shock and outrage. A handful of freckles, the only marks on her porcelain complexion, stood out in sharp relief on her small nose.

She wasn't the only one his declaration had surprised. Chance had been shocked himself when he had first offered to help the boy. And he was shocked now to find himself so determined to keep that promise. Hopefully this would be a promise he could keep, unlike the one he'd made to a boy in Afghanistan.

"This isn't any of your business," she continued, her green eyes bright with anger.

"Your son made it my business when he asked for my help," Chance pointed out. The little boy had done more than that; his vulnerability had reached the protective father in Chance.

"He doesn't need your help," she insisted.

"Then you're going to tell him what he wants to know?" He suspected the mother was just as stubborn as the son.

She nodded. "When he's old enough to understand."

"I'm thirty-three and can't understand why anyone

would keep a father and son apart," he said. Robyn wasn't just punishing him, unless he had been gone so long that his son really didn't want anything to do with him anymore.

Jessie lifted her chin in the gesture her child emulated. "Tommy doesn't have a father."

"You're young. You were only seventeen when you had your child. As a minor, you wouldn't have been able to go to a sperm bank or been allowed to serve as a surrogate."

"You didn't learn all that from interrogating my son," she said, eyes narrowing with suspicion and anger. "You checked me out."

"I pulled up your driver's license," he admitted. "I had to verify Tommy had given me the correct address." It wasn't the only reason he'd checked her out. He'd wanted to make sure that little boy, so desperate for his help, didn't also need his protection. But Chance hadn't found so much as a parking ticket on Jessie Phillips; no one had ever filed a complaint against her, not a teacher or a neighbor.

"He did. He's home safe and sound. You can leave now." Her voice was as cold as the glare she directed at him. "And you shouldn't have made him a promise you won't be able to keep."

He agreed. Silently. He personally knew the pain of broken promises and didn't want Tommy Phillips to have to experience that hurt. "What makes you so certain I can't keep that promise?"

"Because you don't know me." Those green eyes flashed a warning and a challenge at him. If she had her way, he wouldn't get to know her. And he wouldn't find out anything about Tommy's father.

His pulse kicked into a quicker pace. Since taking on the job of Forest Glen's sheriff two months ago, he hadn't even had a speeder challenge a ticket. He'd told himself that was what he wanted, peace and quiet and a safe environment after two tours of duty and years on the Chicago police force before that. But Tommy's mother, with her red hair and eyes bright with anger, disrupted his peace in a way that had his muscles tensing and his breath coming faster and harder. "So you're not going to tell me anything."

She shook her head again, her lips pressed tightly together—the same way Tommy had responded to her questions. Like the red hair, her son had definitely inherited his stubbornness from her. But from whom had he inherited his pale blue eyes?

"Hey, Jessie," a man called out, drawing Chance's attention. A skinny guy with thinning brown hair stood on the sidewalk.

Chance had been so focused on her that he'd barely noticed the neighbor walking up. Two months as the sheriff of a sedate town must have dulled his reflexes.

"Everything all right?" the man asked with a friendly smile.

Jessie nodded. "Yes, Bruce. Thanks for checking."

"Tommy's not in any trouble, is he, Sheriff?" Bruce walked down the short sidewalk to climb the stairs to the porch.

"No," Chance assured the nosy neighbor. Something else he had to get used to in a small town was how everyone was always in everyone else's business. Of course Jessie Phillips probably figured he fit in just fine. What she told her son about his father really was her business, and he had no legal reason to butt into the situation. But the kid's plea for help had gotten to him on a whole other level, had reached the father in him more than the lawman.

"The boy came into the office is all," Chance explained to the man, who was obviously waiting for more information.

"He has wanted to meet you for a while," the guy said. "So have I." He held out a hand.

"Excuse me, please," Jessie said as the men shook. She pulled open the bright red front door of her house and stepped inside. "I need to talk to Tommy."

"Bruce Johnson." The neighbor introduced himself to Chance, sparing a quick glance at the door closing behind Tommy's mother. "You're sure everything's okay?"

Chance nodded. "Yeah…"

Except that he doubted Jessie would open the door to him unless he served her with a search warrant, and he had no grounds to request one. No judge would consider Chance's promise to a young boy probable cause. He'd have to find another way to keep his promise, like persuading the mother to talk to her son. He'd glimpsed the fear in her eyes and suspected she was as scared as she was defensive. Why? What was Jessie Phillips's story?

"Let me know if you need anything," Bruce said. "I know what it's like to be new to town. My wife and I moved here just last year."

Chance smiled in appreciation of the offer. "Forest Glen seems like a nice place to live."

"Great place," Bruce assured him. "Especially if you have a family."

Chance didn't.

Not anymore.

JESSIE GLARED at the shadow the sheriff cast through her living room window onto the hardwood floor. His deep voice rumbled through the leaded glass as he and Bruce continued their conversation on her front porch. How dare he…how dare he bring back all her guilt and regrets and fears?

"You're really mad, huh?" Tommy asked, his voice barely louder than a whisper as he hesitated in the archway between the tiny living room and tinier dining room.

Yes. At herself and the handsome sheriff. "I'm not mad at you."

"You're not?" he asked, his brows drawn together in skepticism.

"Well, you shouldn't have gone into town alone on your bike," she admonished him.

"It's only a couple blocks farther than Christopher's house," he said.

She shook her head. "You can't go *anywhere* without asking my permission first."

"You would have told me no," he pointed out—correctly. Tommy was much too smart for her peace of mind. "You wouldn't have let me file a police report."

"No, I wouldn't have," she agreed. "Your not having a dad is not a crime."

"I have a dad," he said. "I'm not stupid. I know where babies come from."

Her mouth dropped open in shock and dread. "How do you know that?"

Just what the heck were they teaching in elementary school nowadays? Of course, knowing Tommy, he had looked it up online. If someone wouldn't, or couldn't, answer one of his questions, he'd find the answer himself. Or ask someone else, such as Sheriff Chance Drayton, to help him. She swallowed a sigh.

"I know storks don't bring babies. And they're not found in cabbage patches, either. It takes a mom and a dad to have a baby. So I know I have a dad. You just won't tell me who he is."

She could have lied to him and claimed that he came from a sperm donor or a test tube. But when he figured out, as the sheriff already had, that she'd been too young when she'd had him for either of those options, Tommy would resent her even more for lying.

If she was going to answer with a lie, she could have gone with an easier one. She could have said his father was dead. When she'd first told him he didn't have one, he'd initially assumed that was the reason and hadn't asked about him again for several years. Until the Johnsons had moved in down the block. Then he'd wanted to know more about his father, and she hadn't been able to let him believe a lie. So she'd clarified that when she'd said he didn't have a dad, she'd meant such a man didn't exist.

"We'll talk about it when you're older," she promised him now. The panic that she'd felt when she'd realized he hadn't gone to the Johnsons returned and pressed heavily on her chest. Her son had been lost to her then, for an excruciating half hour, until the sheriff had brought him home to her. If she told Tommy about his dad, she risked losing him again. Maybe permanently…

"You always say that," he griped. "It's not fair. I'm old now."

The panic increased, shortening her breath. He was growing up too fast, much faster than she'd realized. Where had her sweet little boy gone? And how much longer could she put off the conversation about his father? He deserved to know the truth.

So she told him at least part of it. "You're not old enough to understand that sometimes things happen between adults and they can't be around each other anymore." Especially when one of them wanted nothing to do with the other…

"I'm not stupid," Tommy said, his voice rising to a shout. "Moms and dads get divorced, but they still get to see their kids."

From the shadow darkening her window and the rumble of those male voices, Jessie was aware that the sheriff and Bruce were still on her porch. She lowered her voice and admitted, "I've never been married, honey."

"Why not?"

She would have had to have been asked, and his father hadn't been about to do that. She forced a smile. "I was too young."

"You, too, huh," he grumbled.

Her lips curved naturally, and she closed the distance between them. "Yes. And I was older than you are now. Just…trust me, okay?"

That was why she hadn't lied to him; she wouldn't deserve his trust if she had.

He studied her, his eyes narrowed. The pale blue color always struck a pang of recognition, loss and regret in her chest. Finally he nodded.

She exhaled a slight breath. "Now it's getting late. I have to heat up our dinner, and after you eat, you need to get to bed. You have school in the morning."

He must have been hungry and tired because he stopped arguing with her. A couple of hours later, long after the sheriff had left her porch, she tucked Tommy into bed. He didn't even squirm as she kissed him good-night and pulled the covers to his chin. Her heart warmed with love for her little boy. "I love you, Tommy."

"Love you, too, Mom," he murmured sleepily, his eyes already closed.

Hours later, Jessie had yet to close her own eyes. And it wasn't because she was studying for the one class she was able to take each semester toward her nursing degree. Nor was she doing laundry. Or dusting. She lay in bed, in the dark, but guilt kept her from sleeping. And the anger that heated her blood whenever she thought of the sheriff's promise to her son.

How dare he presume to do…what she should have done herself? She loved her son, so why did she keep denying him the thing he most wanted—his father? Resigned to not sleeping, she snapped on the Tiffany lamp beside the bed and pulled open one of the drawers of the mission-style table beneath it. After pushing aside some books and papers, she removed a small box wallpapered in faded rose-colored taffeta from an old prom dress.

With her fingers trembling, she lifted out a letter that, like her son, was eight years old. She hadn't read it that often over the years, but she remembered what it said. And every time she began to doubt herself, she read it again.

Dear Jess,

I'm so glad you aren't pregnant. Us having a baby would've been a huge mistake. We're too young and have too much living left to do. I think my folks are right. We got too serious too soon. And with me away at school now, it's not working out anymore. It's too hard on both of us trying to keep a long-distance relationship going. We really need to end it. You might be mad now, but you'll thank me later.

Keith

Would he thank her now—if he learned that she'd lied to him? Back then, reading that letter and realizing how he'd felt, she had been glad that she'd lied about the pregnancy. But with Tommy desperately wanting a dad, she worried now that she'd made the wrong decision all those years ago. Yet trying to fix it at this point could cost her everything.

"So why'd the sheriff bring you home?" Christopher asked as Tommy settled onto the bus seat next to him.

Tommy shrugged off his backpack and dropped it onto the floor next to a wad of hard blue gum. "I didn't break the law or anything," he said. "I just wanted the sheriff to help me with something."

"Is he as cool as everybody says?" Christopher asked,

his voice all crackly as if he were really excited. "Does he have scars and tattoos like the army guys do?"

Tommy shrugged. After seeing his friend playing ball with his dad yesterday, he'd been too mad to really think about meeting the ex-Marine. He should be able to play catch with his own dad, not have to borrow someone else's. He had a dad, out there somewhere, maybe. He wasn't dead, like Tommy had thought all those years. Well, his mom had said that the guy wasn't dead when Tommy was born, but that was all she'd finally told him.

So why wasn't he around?

Christopher nudged him. "So?"

Remembering the sheriff's promise to help him, he nodded. "Yeah, he's really cool."

"Too bad *he* wasn't your dad, huh? He could tell you war stories and maybe he'd let you turn on the siren in his car."

Tommy drew in a breath that puffed out his chest a little bit and replied, "He did."

Christopher's eyes opened wide behind his glasses. "You got to use the siren?"

Other kids—older kids—turned around in their seats and leaned out into the aisle, wanting to know what he and his friend were talking about. Usually they never paid any attention to the younger kids except to try to trip them in the aisle.

"He let me use the siren and the lights," Tommy said. He didn't mention that it was only in the parking lot of the tiny police department. But it was still cool. And maybe those older kids would think he was cool, too.

"Were you in a car chase?" Christopher asked, his voice all squeaky again.

Tommy glanced at the older kids. He wanted to lie. But his mom had a real strict no-lying rule, so he shook his head. "Nah. The sheriff said that nobody speeds in this town."

"It's boring," someone said.

"Probably really boring to him after the stuff he's done," his friend remarked.

"He's got a purple heart," another boy commented. "My dad saw it."

Purple heart? Tommy couldn't figure how someone would have seen the sheriff's heart. It wasn't like he had a zipper down his chest—unless he'd been blown up a little bit by a bomb. He'd have to ask to see his scars and tattoos next time they saw each other. The sheriff had promised he'd stay in touch; something about keeping Tommy "prized" of his investigation.

Tommy had figured the prize would be getting to finally meet his dad. But maybe the prize was getting to know Sheriff Drayton.

Too bad his mom didn't seem to like the guy. But maybe she just had to get to know him. And if the sheriff kept coming around because he was helping Tommy, she could get to know him better.

Maybe he'd show her his scars, too.

Chapter Three

Moms and dads get divorced, but they still get to see their kids.

Tommy Phillips's words, shouted at his mother, had been ringing in Chance's head ever since he'd eavesdropped on their conversation. He hadn't meant to overhear. He hadn't meant to stick around so long after Jessie Phillips had slammed the door on him, but Bruce Johnson was a friendly man and kept talking. And talking. But not so loudly that Chance hadn't overheard the kid's part of the conversation going on inside the house. And wished like hell that he hadn't. He blew out a ragged breath. "Oh, Tommy..."

Chance couldn't even remember being that young and that certain that life was fair. Tommy had no idea what the world was really like, and he hoped the boy never had to learn. Remembering the fear in her pretty green eyes, he wondered...was that why Jessie Phillips wouldn't tell her son who his father was? Was she only trying to protect her child?

That was the excuse Robyn had used when she'd filed for full custody of their son. She was only trying to protect Matthew. From Chance? He would never hurt his son. Not intentionally. It had upset Matthew when

Chance was deployed to Afghanistan. But Robyn had been the reason he'd stayed in the reserves after his initial stint in the Marines—to help pay for her college and med school loans. And to show her appreciation, she'd taken away his son. He uttered another sigh, ragged with frustration.

Robyn had no reason to protect their son from Chance. But did Jessie Phillips have to protect Tommy?

"Tired? Here's some coffee to perk you up." Eleanor placed a steaming cup of the aromatic, black brew on his desk.

"You don't need to bring me coffee," he reminded her. He was perfectly capable of getting his own. "But thank you."

She smiled. "You're welcome. You're going to have to get used to it. I'm too old to retrain myself. Sheriff Beuker always had to have his coffee. 'Course the caffeine was probably the only thing keeping him awake."

"Lucky guy," Chance murmured as he took a sip of the hot, strong drink and nodded in appreciation. He had so many things that kept him awake: memories of the past, worries for the future, and now that damn promise he'd made to Tommy Phillips to find his father. Tommy's mother was right; it wasn't a promise he'd had any business making.

"Sheriff Beuker slept like an infant," Eleanor remarked with a smile, "with all the nodding off he did throughout the day."

"It's been a while, but I don't remember infants sleeping all that much." Matthew hadn't. Even as a baby, he'd had boundless energy. His son needed more room to run around and play than the cramped apartment in Chicago and the crowded city street outside it.

"Well, *he* slept without a care in the world," she amended with a chuckle.

The last time Chance had had no cares, he must have been a child. A weary sigh slipped from his lips, and he leaned back in his chair.

"I thought I heard you talking to yourself a little while ago," Eleanor said, settling into the low-backed leather chair in front of his desk. It wasn't that she had to stay at hers; the phone hardly ever rang. And the only recent visitor had been Tommy. "Beuker always rambled away to himself, but that was because he was getting senile. What has you talking to yourself, Sheriff Drayton?"

"Chance," he reminded her.

She smiled again but shook her head. "Sheriff."

Two months he'd worked with the woman, and she still refused to use his first name. He pushed his hand through his hair.

"You have a lot to talk about," she prodded him, "with everything you have going on."

While he hadn't specifically shared his personal problems with her, she must have taken enough calls from his lawyer that she'd figured out exactly what was going on in his life.

"It's actually Tommy Phillips who's weighing on my mind," he admitted, disgusted with himself for making that promise to the boy. Had he done it because he really wanted to find Tommy's dad for him or because he couldn't be a dad to his own son?

He suspected it was the latter. But just because he hadn't had the most altruistic motive behind his promise didn't mean he didn't intend to keep it. He had even gone so far as to pull up the boy's birth certificate from county records. But Tommy's father was listed as unknown. Gauging from her reaction when Chance had passed on her son's request, Jessie Phillips seemed to have every intention of keeping it that way. Hopefully she had a damn good reason. Better than Robyn's...

And if she did, he'd have to break his promise to Tommy. Hell, even if she didn't, Jessie Phillips was still the boy's mother. What she told her son about his father was her decision. Not Chance's.

"That little guy really got to you," Eleanor mused, staring thoughtfully at him. She had definitely figured out exactly *why* the boy had gotten to him. But then in addition to the calls, she had to have noticed Matthew's picture on his desk. In the photo, a class portrait from a couple of years ago, he looked around Tommy's age. And with his dark hair and navy blue eyes, he looked like Chance.

"Tommy Phillips wants a relationship with his dad," he said, hoping his son wanted the same thing with him. "And he's too young to understand we can't always get what we want." He grimaced as the coffee turned acidic in his stomach. "I shouldn't have made that promise to him."

"No, you shouldn't have," Eleanor agreed with the simple honesty on which Chance had come to rely.

"I did swear to protect and serve the people of Forest Glen, though," he reminded her.

"Yes, you did," Eleanor agreed. "Mrs. Wilson is one of those people, and she still hasn't found that cat yet."

"I thought Steven went out yesterday to look for it," he said, referring to the younger of the two deputies.

Eleanor shook her head. "No. His allergies are so bad he can't even get out of his vehicle at her place."

Chance set aside the mug of coffee and stood up. "I'll head out there and look around for her." Maybe he'd be able to find at least one thing that had been reported missing.

"Are you allergic?" she asked.

He shook his head. "No." Robyn had had a cat. Of course the creature had hated Chance so much it hardly ever came near him. Robyn must have grown to hate him as much as her cat had, because if she'd had any feeling left for him, she wouldn't be keeping him from his son.

"Be careful," Eleanor advised him as he headed out the door.

He suppressed a grin at her mothering. He'd made it through two tours of duty in Afghanistan without a physical scratch. He doubted anything would happen to him while looking for a cat.

"JESS, CAN YOU STAY a little while longer?" Dr. Malewitz asked just as she'd pulled her purse from the bottom drawer of the metal desk in the tiny reception area of the single-physician medical practice. "Reception" consisted of her desk and half a dozen orange vinyl chairs, a coffee table and an overstuffed magazine rack. The gray-haired doctor leaned out the door of one of the three exam rooms. "I have a new patient coming in."

Jessie glanced at the appointment book that lay open on the leather blotter. Dr. Malewitz was an old-fashioned physician who preferred the ledger to the computer system she'd set up for him. "But there are no more appointments written down."

"That's why I need you to stay and start a chart for him," the doctor explained. "Can you have someone else meet Tommy's bus today?"

"Of course," she said.

"No, you can leave, and I'll start the chart," Ruth Malewitz offered as she slipped out of one of the other exam rooms.

Jessie smiled but shook her head. The doctor's wife, a registered nurse, already picked up too much of her slack, handling the tasks Jessie couldn't complete since she only worked the hours Tommy was at school. But Ruth insisted that motherhood came first.

"I'll stay," Jessie said. "It's no problem. I'll ask Brenda Johnson to watch him until I get home." She'd just put down the phone from calling her neighbor when the exterior door opened and the new patient walked into the reception area.

Breaths wheezed and rattled in Sheriff Drayton's muscular chest as he stumbled through the door, his eyes probably too swollen to see where he was going. She could barely detect a glint of that deep blue between his red eyelids. "Are you all right?" she asked, leaping up from her chair and coming around her desk.

"I…I c-can't breathe," he gasped.

Mrs. Wilson stepped inside the open door. "He must be like that deputy of his—allergic to my cats," she said with a disapproving click of her tongue against her false teeth. "I called Doc Mal, so he'd have the shot ready for him." The white-haired woman, her sweater coated with cat hair, pushed him forward so that he stumbled against Jessie.

She wrapped her arm around his waist as he wound his around her shoulders. His labored breathing stirred her hair. "Dr. Malewitz!" she shouted.

But the older man was already there, grabbing the sheriff's other arm to help him into the exam room. Ruth stood inside the room; she held a needle in a latex-gloved hand. "Any allergies to antihistamines?"

"I—I don't know," he murmured. "I…I didn't think I was allergic to c-cats…"

"I should take his medical history," Jessie said, "before you give him anything. I could try to get his records from his attending physician."

"There's no time," Dr. Malewitz said, his stethoscope pressed against Chance Drayton's chest. "He's going to lose his airway."

"Th-throat's closing," Chance choked out between gasps for air.

Still pressed against his side, Jessie trembled. But then Dr. Malewitz pulled the sheriff away from her and helped him onto the paper-draped exam table. "We've got this, Jess…"

Dismissed, she backed toward the door, her steps slow and heavy with her reluctance to leave. Dr. Malewitz was just a small-town physician. He handled colds, earaches and other viruses. For anything more serious, patients went to the hospitals or specialists in Grand Rapids or Muskegon.

Bumping into Mrs. Wilson in the doorway to the exam room, she turned to the older woman, dubbed the crazy cat lady by most of Forest Glen. "You should have called an ambulance," she said.

"Figured it'd be quicker to bring him here. I drove that fancy new police car of his, lights flashing and everything." The woman's eyes glinted with excitement. "I got him here real *fast*."

Jessie glanced back inside the exam room, but Ruth shut the door before she could see more than a glimpse of his bare chest as he dragged off his shirt. Her breath caught with a gasp.

Hopefully Mrs. Wilson had gotten him there soon enough.

"I FEEL LIKE hell," Chance answered in reply to Jessie Phillips's question. His throat was sore and scratchy, like his eyes. And his head pounded. "But I could have driven myself home."

She laughed. "How? You can barely see."

"The swelling's gone down since the shot," he replied. But water streamed from his eyes now, probably because of all the cat hair Mrs. Wilson had left on the driver's seat. He preferred Jessie Phillips behind the wheel; he trusted her more than he had the older woman.

Not that he had anything against Mrs. Wilson's age. The woman definitely had all her faculties and then some. When he'd started wheezing in her barn full of cats, she'd responded by driving him immediately to the doctor's office. She'd just enjoyed that drive a little too much as she'd sped, lights flashing and siren wailing, down the rural roads leading from her farmhouse into town. Remembering how the tires had spun on the gravel, the car fishtailing and nearly careening into the ditch, Chance grimaced. Even without the allergic reaction, he would have had trouble breathing, the way she'd been driving.

Jessie, on the other hand, drove slowly and carefully, as if she were afraid that any sudden turn might have him gasping again. "I'm going to be a real cool mom now that I've driven the police car," she pointed out.

With her red hair bound high in a ponytail, she looked more like a teenager than a mother. And despite working in an office, she'd dressed casually—in jeans and a bright pink sweater that made her look even younger.

"I know what else would make Tommy think you're a cool mom," he said.

The smile left Jessie's beautiful face as her delicate jaw tensed. "You need to let this drop. It's not any of your business."

"True," he admitted. "But will Tommy let it go?"

"He was fine last night after you left," she assured him. "And he was his usual happy self this morning."

"So you think he already forgot about it?" Could a kid who, just yesterday, had been as determined as Tommy Phillips give up so easily? While the boy had seemed far older, he was still just eight. A kid. Maybe since he'd only been able to e-mail and chat on the phone with Matthew the past year, and was denied any visitation, Chance had forgotten how a child's mind worked. Would his son forget about him this easily?

Jessie nodded but spared him a glance that revealed her own doubts. "For now."

"Do you want me to talk to him?" he offered. Take back his promise? He wasn't sure he could do that, though, if he looked into Tommy's hopeful, vulnerable eyes again.

Jessie must have realized that because she shook her head again. "No, like I said, he's fine now. Let's just forget all about this."

If only he could...

But he wanted to know why Jessie had listed her

baby's father as unknown. Unless she'd been a real wild teenager, he doubted that she didn't know her son's paternity. So if she knew, why would she have omitted to name Tommy's dad? Had she been afraid of him? Was she still?

Chance had glimpsed that fear in her eyes when he'd told her what Tommy wanted from him. But she didn't act like the battered women he'd met during his years in law enforcement in Chicago. She didn't shy away from him as if afraid to be touched. In fact, she'd reached for him back at the doctor's office, wrapping her arm around him. To help him.

After she'd left the exam room, the doctor and nurse had sung her praises about how she juggled her work and nursing school schedule around Tommy's. That as hard a worker as she was, she was a better mother. So why had she refused the boy a relationship with his father? Maybe if he knew her reasons he could understand Robyn's better. Not forgive—never forgive—but at least understand…

He opened his mouth, but a cough smothered the questions he wanted to ask. By the time the spasm passed, she'd pulled the car into his driveway. Even if he hadn't given his address to her for those medical records, she had probably known where he lived. He doubted there were any secrets in this town but hers.

"Do you have anyone who can check on you?" she asked.

He shook his head but couldn't quite shake off the loneliness that tugged at him. The only person he'd known in Forest Glen had died while he'd been deployed the first time. Grandma Drayton, aware of how much he'd loved the summers he'd spent with her, had left him this house. In the middle of a five-acre lot, the Victorian farmhouse sat back from the tree-lined road. The freshly budded leaves on the tall oaks in the yard cast shadows across the wraparound porch. He'd fixed its worn floorboards, but he needed to replace some of the spindles in the decorative railing. The teal and purple trim clashed with the warm yellow siding. Grandma had loved her bright colors, and he couldn't quite bring himself to repaint the house. Hell, if things didn't work out the way he wanted, he might not even be able to continue living here.

"I can't stay," she said. "I've already left Tommy at the Johnsons' too long. I don't want to interfere with any of their plans for the evening."

"I haven't asked you to stay," he pointed out, though he was tempted to do just that. He wanted to talk to her, but while the antihistamines had reduced the swelling, his lids were heavy with drowsiness, which was probably why Dr. Malewitz had insisted on Jessie driving him home. With his senses muddled, it was safer for him if she wasn't around because he might forget everything but how beautiful she was.

Especially now as color flushed her face, darkening her pale skin to nearly the same shade as those sparse freckles on her nose. "I know you haven't," she said. "But I don't think you should be left alone."

He snorted at the notion; since the divorce, that was all he knew. Hell, even before the divorce he'd been alone, except for Matthew, because he and Robyn had been so busy with their separate lives and goals. "I'm used to it. I'll be fine."

"You don't have to be all by yourself," she said.

Maybe it was the antihistamines, but an impulse to

tease her overcame him. He leaned across the console, suppressing a grin as her eyes widened in surprise at his nearness. Then he lowered his voice and murmured, "I thought you had to go home…"

She nodded then jerked back when her face nearly touched his. "I—I do. I—I wasn't talking about me."

He might have intended to tease her, but with her lips so close to his, he was the one fighting to breathe now. And he suspected it had nothing to do with the allergy attack. He leaned away from her.

"Mrs. Wilson," Jessie said, blurting the name out with a breath she'd apparently been holding. "She's the one who offered to come back and sit with you."

The nurse had taken the older woman home to check on the cat Chance had found caught in the tractor in the barn. He glanced down at the deep scratches on his forearm and winced as he remembered how deeply the feline's claws had sunk into his skin when he'd tried working it free of the rusty tractor frame.

"That was nice of her to offer," he said, especially as he suspected the brusque old woman preferred her cats to humans. And because she did, her hair-covered clothes would set back his recovery. "But unnecessary." He pushed open the door and had to use the frame to lever himself from the seat. Fighting for breath had sapped his strength. "I'll send one of the deputies over to your place to collect the car in a little while."

"I'll leave it and walk," she said, turning off the ignition. "It's not far."

He'd noticed the night before that his house was only a couple of blocks from the little Craftsman bungalow she and Tommy called home. This place, despite his fond memories of childhood summers spent at his grandmother's, was still just a house. It wouldn't be a home until his son was able to move in with him.

He shifted his focus back to the woman now standing on her side of the sedan. "But how will Tommy know how cool you are unless he sees you driving the car?"

A smile curved her lips again. "Forest Glen is a small town. He'll find out."

Chance had only spent a couple of weeks here each of those long ago summers, and he'd loved the sense of freedom and security in the quiet country. The rest of his life he'd lived in Chicago—except for the two tours he'd spent in war zones. Hell, before he'd been deployed his marriage had become a war zone.

"You're saying everyone knows everyone else's business?" he asked, wondering how long Eleanor would keep his secret.

She must have misunderstood his question because her voice cracked with anger as she warned him, "Don't you dare ask around about me…about Tommy's father." Her cheeks flamed with embarrassment. She slammed the driver's side door. "You can't. You have no legal right to pry into my life."

Maybe all his years on the Chicago force had made him cynical, or his divorce had left him so bitter that he wanted to believe she was doing something wrong. But he had no evidence of a crime, so no reason to investigate her.

"I won't," he assured her. He wouldn't ask around; he wouldn't make her the topic of speculation and gossip because that wouldn't just affect her. It would affect her son, too.

"You wouldn't learn anything if you did," she said, as

if she didn't trust him to keep his word. "No one knows my business but me."

He grinned at her naiveté. "I can't imagine anyone who's grown up in a small town can keep anything about her life secret."

"I didn't grow up here." She shrugged. "Well, in a way I did. But I wasn't born here. I moved here after I was already pregnant with Tommy. So no one knows…"

"Father unknown," he murmured.

She gasped. "You looked at his birth certificate!"

Regret increased the pounding in his head. Even as he'd pulled up the record, he'd known he was overstepping. And he knew why. He could have shared his own situation with Jessie, but like her, he didn't want everybody discovering his secrets. "Why don't you want anyone to find out who Tommy's father is?" If the man was a threat, Chance had to know. It was his job to protect her and Tommy. "Is he dangerous?"

She shook her head, anger flashing in her eyes. "You're the one who's dangerous. You're disrupting my life. Digging into my private records, making promises to my son…" Her eyes glistened now with tears.

Chance swallowed a groan of regret. She was right. "I'm sorry."

"You should be sorry!" she yelled at him. "You had no right!" Then she turned away and stomped off down his driveway.

Even though breathing was still an effort, he could have chased after her. But he'd already apologized. If he'd caught her, he might have done something stupid— something like he'd been tempted to do in the car when he'd leaned so close to her that their mouths had nearly touched.

Staring after Jessie Phillips, he had to remind himself that the only relationship he was interested in was with his son. After his disastrous divorce, he could never trust any woman again, and especially not one whose behaviour reminded him so much of his ex. Jessie Phillips would not tempt him again.

Chapter Four

What must he think of her? Did he actually believe she didn't know who had fathered Tommy? That she'd slept around so much she'd had no idea?

Heat rushed to her face, and she fanned herself with her hand as she kicked off her tangled blankets. She'd like to blame her temperature on the unusually warm spring weather rather than embarrassment. That would imply she cared what Sheriff Chance Drayton thought of her. And she didn't.

She didn't care what anyone thought but Tommy. And he'd totally dropped the subject of his father, not asking her one question in the week since he'd filed his missing person report with the sheriff. He was over it—for now. Why couldn't she let it go?

It was Saturday, and she should have been snuggled under the blankets sleeping in. But instead, she'd tossed and turned since dawn. Early morning sunlight streamed through her blinds, but she closed her eyes again. The house was quiet. Maybe she could catch some sleep now.

But just then a crash reverberated throughout the house. She jumped from her bed and ran down the hall to Tommy's room. "What happened? Are you okay?"

Since he didn't have bunk beds, the noise wouldn't have been so loud if he had fallen out of bed. The times it had happened before, his small body tumbling onto the floor had resulted in a dull thud and a murmured oath from him. Her hand trembling, she flipped on the light, which glinted off ceramic shards on the hardwood floor.

Tommy sat cross-legged next to the remains of his broken piggy bank, a hammer against his knee. "That was loud, huh?" he remarked, his light blue eyes bright with excitement.

"Uh, yeah," Jessie replied. "What are you doing? Why'd you break open piggy?"

"I need to buy another baseball mitt," he said as he unfolded crumpled bills and stacked coins. "Can you take me to Smith's Sporting Goods?"

"It doesn't open for a few hours yet," she pointed out. "And I doubt you need another glove already." He wasn't growing that fast, not fast enough to have outgrown the one she'd bought him two Christmases ago.

"But I gotta have two."

"Why?" she asked.

He lowered his gaze to the pile of coins. "I just do…" His mouth tightened into that little stubborn line she knew so well. Asking him any other questions would be pointless.

"After breakfast," she said, "we'll go into town and check out the sales at Smith's." If she could afford it, she tried to give Tommy what he asked for, especially since he usually asked for so little. Except the one thing she couldn't risk giving him…

"DO I NEED TO COME to Chicago?" Chance asked as he paced the sidewalk outside the storefronts on Main Street.

"We don't have a hearing with the judge yet," Trenton Sanders replied. "All the meetings have been between your ex's lawyer, me and the mediator."

"Maybe that's the problem," Chance said. "Maybe I just need to talk to Robyn myself."

"She refuses to talk to you or let you speak with the boy anymore," the lawyer reminded him, his voice rough with the same impatience that tore Chance up inside.

When he'd filed for full custody, Robyn had cut off all communication between him and Matthew. At least when he was in Afghanistan, he'd been able to talk to his son through letters and e-mails when he'd had Internet access.

"She's being unreasonable." He never would have believed the smart, funny woman he'd married so many years ago could be so bitter and spiteful. Especially when he'd done nothing to deserve her anger. Like he'd promised his son, he'd come home from Afghanistan without a scratch. He glanced down at the ridges of healing skin on his arm. All those years as a police officer and then a detective in Chicago, he'd never been hurt, either. Until a damn cat took him out in sleepy Forest Glen.

"The mediator has told her lawyer that she's being unreasonable and that's what she'll report to the judge. Then we'll get a custody hearing scheduled, and you'll need to come to Chicago for that."

Chance expelled a ragged sigh of relief. "Good. When will all this happen?"

A sigh rattled through the phone, echoing his. "Her lawyer asked for the chance to confer with her client and then meet with the mediator one last time before it's turned over to the judge."

"It's just another delaying tactic," Chance argued. "Robyn and her lawyer have been dragging this out for months now—months I'm losing of my son's life."

"I know. I'm sorry."

"Really?" he challenged Trenton. He couldn't unleash his temper on the person he was actually angry with, since she refused to talk to him. "All these delays are adding hours to my bill. Hell, I should go. Every minute I talk to you is costing me."

"Damn it, Chance, that's not fair, and you know it," his former platoon sergeant and long-time friend reminded him. "Hell, I don't even want to bill you. You're the one insisting on paying me."

"Yeah," Chance said, glancing into the window of the store as he paced in front of it. His attention was drawn to the bright red hair of the only two customers. "I don't want to owe you."

"Hey, I'm the one who owes you, and I'll never be able to pay you back."

"Try," he urged his friend. "Get my son back for me, and we'll be even." He clicked off the cell phone without another word, just as Jessie Phillips lifted her head and met his gaze through the store window. He'd rather not have to deal with her right now, not when he was so mad at Robyn for doing the same thing to him that Jessie might be doing to Tommy's dad.

But it was too late for him to escape. Tommy had already seen Chance and the little boy tugged free of his mom's hand on his shoulder and rushed out the door. "Sheriff Drayton! Sheriff Drayton!"

"Hey, Tommy."

The little boy grabbed Chance's hand, wrapping both of his around it. "I need your help!"

Chance swallowed a groan. Damn. The kid hadn't given up. "I'm sorry. I haven't been able to find—"

"Sheriff!" Jessie called out his title now as she joined them on the sidewalk. Standing behind her son, she directed a pointed stare at Chance; her green-eyed gaze was very intense. Her hair was loose around her shoulders now, but made her look no older than the ponytail had. "That's not what he wants help with."

He released a shallow breath in relief. "Okay then. What do you need?"

Tommy tugged on Chance's hand, pulling him toward the open door of the sporting goods store. "I need your 'pinion."

"I'm sure the sheriff is very busy, Tommy," Jessie said, easing her son away from Chance. "He doesn't have time to go shopping with us."

Something shifted in his chest at the image Jessie's words conjured in his mind: a happy family hanging out together. He'd always hated shopping, though, and so had Matthew. They would have rather been out playing sports than buying the equipment for them.

"He's just standing out here," Tommy pointed out. "He's not doing anything."

"He's the sheriff," Jessie reminded her son. "He's always working." She glanced to the cell phone he clutched in his palm. Maybe she'd seen him on it, arguing with his lawyer.

She'd been inside the store, so she wouldn't have been

able to overhear any of his conversation, which was good. Since she wouldn't share her secrets, he wouldn't be thrilled if she learned his, especially since she would realize why he might not be entirely objective about Tommy being denied a relationship with his dad.

"Actually I was just having lunch with the mayor and had to step out to take a call," he said. "I should probably rejoin him." But when he glanced back toward the diner two buildings down, the mayor was walking out with a couple of old cronies. Mayor Applegate lifted his hand in a wave at Chance, and then slid behind the wheel of his vintage pickup truck.

"That's not going to work," she murmured. With a slight nudge, she urged Tommy, "Go back inside and we'll meet you there in a minute."

"What's not going to work?" Chance asked, wary of being left alone with her. Even though he didn't agree with or understand the woman, she fascinated him.

"Your excuse to escape," she replied with an unlady-like snort of disgust. "It's not going to work."

"What makes you think I want to escape?"

"You don't exactly look like you're in the mood for shopping," she said, her eyes narrowed as she studied his face. "In fact, you look pretty mad right now."

She couldn't have overheard his conversation but she'd definitely picked up on his reaction to it.

"I'm fine with this," Chance insisted. "I thought you were the one who might have a problem with my hanging out with Tommy."

"You're not hanging out with my son," she said. "You're going in there and giving your—"

"'Pinion?"

"Yes." Her anger with him a few days ago was

apparently forgotten now, and she smiled. "That's all he wants."

She wasn't just lying to her son; she was probably lying to herself, too, if she actually believed that.

TOMMY STARED at the couple standing on the sidewalk outside the door. His mom looked pretty and really young, just like some of the girls on the bus when she smiled brightly like she was now. And the sheriff looked tall, and a little mean, with his eyes all serious and his jaw real hard-looking. But then he walked through the door and smiled at Tommy.

And Tommy's stomach flipped with nerves and a rush of hope and maybe the flapjacks his mom had made him that morning. Too bad the sheriff wasn't his dad. But if he was, he would have said something when Tommy told him who he was looking for.

Was he trying to find Tommy's dad like he'd promised? Or had Mom talked him out of it? Maybe that was why she'd wanted to get rid of Tommy and speak to the sheriff alone.

He rushed forward and grabbed the man's big hand, pulling him toward the baseball stuff in the middle of the cluttered sporting goods store. His mom would have had a fit if he'd kept his room as messy as the store was. Stuff overflowed crates and was falling off the shelves. With his free hand, Tommy grabbed a glove and held it out to the sheriff. "See if it fits."

Sheriff Drayton pulled his hand away from Tommy's and slid it into the glove. "It's a little snug for me," he said. "Probably would be big for you, though."

"He already has a glove," his mom said. "I'm not sure why he thinks he needs another one. But then I know nothing about baseball, at least not enough to give him the 'pinion he wants about the glove."

"I was the catcher on my high school team, and we were undefeated," Sheriff Drayton said with a grin. "But that seems like a long time ago now."

"Catcher," Tommy said. That dream he'd been having about playing catch with his dad became a little clearer than it usually was. Instead of throwing a ball at a shadow, the guy had a face. It was Chance Drayton's.

The sheriff picked up another glove from the table and slid his hand into the leather. Then he scooped up a ball and chucked it hard—like so hard it would have stung Tommy's hand—into the glove. "This one feels good."

"I'll buy that one, then," Tommy said, shoving his hand in his pocket for the roll of bills and the bunch of coins he'd taken from his broken piggy bank.

"But it'll be way too big for you, for at least a few more years," the sheriff said as he tugged off the glove.

"It's not for me," Tommy explained. "It's for my dad."

"Your dad?" His mom's voice went all squeaky like Christopher's did.

"Yeah, the sheriff promised to find him," Tommy reminded them both. "When my dad comes here to see me, I wanna have a glove for him, so we can play catch like Christopher and his dad do."

The sheriff sighed. "Tommy..."

His mom held up a hand as if to stop the man from saying anything else. "I've got this." She crouched down so that her face was level with Tommy's. "The sheriff is not going to find your dad."

"I knew it." Tommy's voice cracked and it was hard to swallow. "I knew you told him not to."

"I shouldn't have offered," the sheriff said. "I should have talked to your mom before I made that promise."

His mom glanced up at the sheriff with a brief smile. "It's a promise he can't keep, honey. But you don't need a dad. You and I have been doing great these last eight years—just the two of us." She straightened up and reached for the gloves on the sporting goods table. "I can get one of these. I can play catch with you."

"No," Tommy snapped. "I don't wanna play catch with a girl."

"I can play catch with you," the sheriff offered. His mom glanced at him again but with a frown instead of a smile this time. "I'll buy this glove for myself." Still holding it, he ran his fingers over the leather. "I've gotten rusty. I could use the practice."

Sure, it would be fun to play catch with the sheriff. Kids might think Tommy was cool if he hung out with the ex-Marine. But still, the guy wasn't his dad no matter how Tommy might wish he was.

Tears stung his eyes, but he blinked them back. He didn't want to look like a baby in front of the sheriff. "You're not gonna find my dad?"

The man glanced at his mom then back at him and shook his head. "I can't."

"But you promised!"

"I shouldn't have done that," Sheriff Drayton said.

Tommy's lip quivered, and he fought to steady it. *Don't cry. Don't cry.*

"No," his mom agreed with the sheriff. "He shouldn't have done that. He doesn't understand the situation."

"You could fix that," the sheriff murmured.

She glared at the man again and crouched down to Tommy's level. "When you're older, I'll explain everything to you," she promised, her voice soft like when she was trying to calm him down after he got hurt or had a bad nightmare. "Right now we should go home. We can play catch."

"I don't wanna play with you," he said again. And not just because she was a girl.

"Tommy," the sheriff began, his hand settling on his shoulder.

But Tommy jerked away. "I don't want to play with you, either. You're a liar!"

"Tommy!" his mother said with a sharp gasp. "You apologize to the sheriff right now for your rudeness."

He shook his head. "You're both liars." And he ran for the door.

"I'll get him," he heard the sheriff offer.

But his mom must have refused because she was the one who caught him outside. He'd only made it a little ways down the block. Since it was just the two of them, he gave in to his tears, letting them run down his face as she wrapped her arms around him.

"I love you, Tommy," she said.

He loved his mom, too. But he wanted it to be more than just the two of them. He wanted it to be like it had been for those few minutes in the store with the sheriff. He wanted a family.

Chapter Five

"Should I tell him the truth?" Jessie asked, able to speak freely since her son wasn't home.

"Who? Chance Drayton or Tommy?" her cousin Belinda asked. The slim blonde kicked off her shoes and curled her legs beneath her on the flower-patterned couch across from Jessie. Only a couple years older than her, Belinda had become more sister than cousin when Jessie had moved in with Belinda's mom, Jessie's aunt, a little over eight years ago.

Jessie knelt on the floor beside the mission-style coffee table, which was littered with the cardboard cartons from their take-out dinner. "Tommy, of course," she said. "I don't care what Chance Drayton thinks."

"You don't?" Belinda arched a brow, then took a sip from her wineglass.

Jessie shook her head and reached for her own glass of dry white wine. "No."

"He's one good-looking man," her cousin said with a wistful sigh.

Jessie couldn't argue that—no woman could miss his deep blue eyes and chiseled features. Not to mention his hard-muscled body. That brief glimpse of his naked chest, lightly dusted with dark hair, was forever burned in her mind.

Belinda laughed. "You've noticed."

"I'd have to be dead not to," she remarked with a disgusted snort at her own weakness. When he'd leaned toward her that day in his car, she'd been tempted to close the distance between them. To kiss him. But after that promise he'd made to Tommy, she should want to kill him instead.

"I know you're not dead, but you've been living like a nun since you moved to Forest Glen," her cousin teased.

"I've been a little busy raising my son," she reminded Belinda. When Tommy had come into the world, after twenty-seven hours of excruciating labor pain, Jessie had promised herself and him that he would always come first with her. She hadn't broken that promise. Or had she? Was not telling him about his dad putting her needs—and her fears—before his?

"You don't have to go it alone, you know."

"So you think I should tell Tommy about his father?" Jessie asked, steering the conversation back to where she'd started it. "Do you think I should tell Tommy's father about him?"

With a heavy sigh, Belinda flopped back on the couch. "I'm not the one you should be asking."

"I want to know what you think."

"You already know what I think, but you pay about as much attention to me as my kids do." Belinda shook her finger at Jessie as if she were chastising one of her children; she had twin seven-year-old girls and a boy just a year younger. She claimed all those grandkids had inspired her mother to move to Florida. But it was love, in the form of the man she'd reunited with, that had compelled Aunt Sue to leave Forest Glen.

Jessie blinked and teased, "Huh? What? Did you say something?"

Belinda chucked a wadded-up napkin at her head. "I thought you were crazy to choose to raise Tommy all alone."

"I wasn't all alone. I had you and Aunt Sue." And she couldn't have endured those miserable months of her pregnancy, the endless hours of labor and the sleepless nights of Tommy's colic without their support. Belinda still helped her with babysitting when Jessie had a night class in Grand Rapids.

"But Tommy's Keith's son, too," Belinda reminded her. "His responsibility. He should have been here to help you. If he'd been paying you child support and helping out, you'd have your nursing degree and you'd be able to buy your own place instead of renting. You wouldn't be just scraping by."

"I'm not just scraping by," Jessie proudly insisted. "I have a good job with flexible hours." Burying a little of her pride, she admitted, "And my parents send me money."

Belinda snorted. "Guilt money for deserting you when you needed them most."

"I could have gone with them." And suffocated under the weight of their disapproval and disappointment in her. She was sure she was the reason they'd wanted to leave Fort Hood, Missouri, because they'd been embarrassed that their teenage daughter had been stupid enough to get pregnant. Jessie hadn't wanted to stay there, either, because she hadn't wanted anyone to notice she was pregnant and tell Keith.

"To live on yet another base, in another country?" Belinda asked.

"Germany," Jessie reminded her. "It's where my mom is from. She has family there." Which was why her parents had decided to retire in the country.

"You and Tommy are their family, too."

"That's why they send money," Jessie said with a smile. "It's fine. I'm happier here in Forest Glen than I was on any of those bases where I grew up. I want to raise my son in one place, too." Not split between two households.

"It must have been hard, growing up like that, switching schools all the time," her cousin commiserated. "Always being the new kid."

She nodded. "It was hard…until I met Keith." Maybe that was why she'd fallen so fast for him, because she hadn't known how long she'd be staying at Fort Hood. Then, ironically, he'd been the one to leave her. "You really think I should have told him?" Jessie swallowed hard. "Do you think I should tell him now?"

"I don't know," her cousin admitted.

"He didn't want me to be pregnant eight years ago. He was relieved when I lied and told him I wasn't." So relieved that he'd dumped her.

"He was eighteen years old," Belinda reminded her.

She shrugged. "But maybe he still doesn't want kids. Then what do I tell Tommy? That his father rejected him twice?"

"Are you afraid of him rejecting Tommy or afraid that he's going to want him?"

Nerves flipped her stomach. Her cousin knew her too well. "That's the other thing. What if he's so pissed that I lied, that I kept him from his son all these years, that he sues me for full custody?"

"No judge would take that boy away from you," Belinda assured her. "You're a great mom. But you might have to share custody. Then you could wind up like me, spending every Wednesday and every weekend alone when Ed and his new bride have my kids."

Jessie had had Tommy all to herself for so long that she didn't know if she could share him. But sharing was the least of her concerns. Despite her cousin's assurances, she wasn't convinced that she wouldn't lose custody of her son.

She shook off her own fears to comfort her cousin, reaching out to pat Belinda's jean-clad knee. "You're always welcome over here." In fact, to keep Belinda from going crazy, they had a standing date every Friday night—until one of them started dating seriously.

"Where's Tommy tonight?" her cousin asked.

"He's sleeping over at his friend Christopher's." Jessie bit her lip, wondering now if that was a good idea. Seeing his friend with his father was what had inspired Tommy's latest quest for information about his own dad.

"The Johnsons, right?" Belinda asked.

"Yes."

"They're a nice family." Belinda emitted a wistful sigh. While she was too proud to admit it, she missed her own family.

"That's what Tommy wants," Jessie said with a sigh of her own. "A family." She wasn't enough for her son anymore. He wanted a father. *His* father.

"Don't we all?" Belinda asked. She'd thought she had it when she'd married her high school sweetheart, but it hadn't lasted. Even though Ed had strayed, Belinda blamed herself for trapping him into marriage when she'd gotten pregnant with the twins.

If Jessie had told Keith the truth, he probably would have insisted on marrying her, too. Then he would have come to resent her as Ed had Belinda. Even when guilt over lying to Keith often kept her awake, Jessie was convinced that she had done the right thing for both of them. But what about Tommy and his longing for a father?

With a sigh, she shrugged off her own problems and focused on her cousin, who was also her best friend. "You should start seriously dating again, Bee," Jessie urged her, squeezing her cousin's knee again.

"I should," Belinda heartily agreed. "Maybe I should go after our new sheriff."

Jessie's stomach flipped. She wanted to blame the greasy, take-out food, but she had a feeling that it was jealousy instead as she imagined Chance Drayton with her beautiful cousin.

"Unless you've already called dibs on him," Belinda said, that brow arched again as she studied Jessie over the rim of her wineglass.

"I—I—of course I haven't…"

Belinda laughed. "Really? Everybody's still talking about you driving his police car. You know what everyone thinks when a man lets a woman drive his car."

"That he just had an allergic reaction and couldn't see to drive himself home?"

"No—" Belinda leaned over and tugged on a lock of Jessie's hair "—that they're involved."

Jessie struggled to hold in a laugh as she lowered her

voice to a conspiratorial whisper. "Then I guess he and Mrs. Wilson must have something going."

Belinda gasped. "Mrs. Wilson? The crazy cat lady?"

"Yeah, she drove his car before I did, so if anyone has dibs on Sheriff Drayton, she does." She sighed in mock resignation.

Belinda dissolved into giggles. "The crazy cat lady and the ex-Marine. Yeah, right…"

It made about as much sense as her and Chance Drayton, Jessie thought. She had absolutely no interest in the man, beyond making certain that he didn't make any more promises to her son that he couldn't keep. She doubted he intended to stay in Forest Glen anyhow; he'd be going back to Chicago someday. Soon, she hoped.

CHANCE COULD BARELY LOOK at his own reflection in the rearview mirror. Tommy Phillips had been right the other day; he was a liar. Well, he hadn't been lying when he'd made that promise to Tommy, but by not keeping that promise, he had become one. He couldn't blame the kid for not wanting to hang out with him, as Chance had offered. Hell, his own kid must not want to spend time with him, or Robyn would have at least agreed to visitation. She loved their son, or so she said when she claimed that she was only trying to protect him.

And right now all Chance had to protect was the citizens of Forest Glen. But not a lot happened here. His allergic reaction was still the talk of the small town. As the story was retold, it got more dramatic. Apparently he'd barely survived the cat attack. He glanced down at the scabbed over scratches on his arm. Damn cat…

But the feline was the only thing that had come close

to breaking the law in Forest Glen. As far as he could determine, Jessie Phillips hadn't. But he was pretty damn certain she knew who Tommy's father was. So why had she lied about his identity on her son's birth certificate?

She'd denied she was in danger—from anyone but Chance. Thoroughly frustrated, he groaned. Hell, maybe he needed to leave it—and her and her son—alone. He had to stop fixating on Jessie and Tommy Phillips. He had to focus instead on his job. And so he returned his attention to the road as he cruised the outskirts of the town square. Since almost everyone was in school or at work, the road was pretty much deserted except for his car and the vehicle ahead of him, which moved so slowly he nearly rear-ended the heavy, metal bumper.

The ancient Cadillac straddled the yellow line now, weaving back and forth across it. He flipped on the lights and sirens. The car slowed, or maybe it continued at the same pace, but it didn't move toward the shoulder of the road. Instead the faded pink Caddy continued to weave across the line.

Thankfully there was no oncoming traffic. Chance hit the lights and siren again but the car did not stop. He reached for the PA and spoke into the mike. "Please, pull off to the shoulder of the road."

But whom was he talking to? Through the rear window, he couldn't even see the top of a head. The driver could have been an elderly person or a kid. He smiled. Hell, maybe it was Tommy Phillips. Maybe Jessie had confiscated his bike, so he'd stolen a car and set off in search of his father himself. Seeing the kid's frustration the other day and knowing his determination, Chance wouldn't put it past him.

"Pull off to the side of the road," he repeated into the mike, his voice echoing on the quiet country road.

Finally brake lights flashed red as the car slowed, then headed toward the shoulder. He pulled behind it at an angle, so that he could walk up to the driver's window without other traffic running him over. More cops got injured in traffic stops than gun battle.

He narrowed his eyes as the brake lights burned red. "Please, put the car in Park," he directed the driver. He didn't want to step from his vehicle only to have the other car flee before he could approach it.

But the car didn't drive off. Instead it backed right into him—with such force than the air bag burst free of the steering wheel and exploded in his face.

"Is SHE okay?" he asked.

Jessie glanced across to where Chance sat in the passenger seat—of her car. Because of the deployed air bag, his had been towed to the body shop.

"Your car?" she asked. She'd had little experience with men; did they assign their vehicles genders?

He shook his head. "No. Mrs. Applegate. Is she all right? She was pretty shaken up when I helped her out of her Cadillac. I was worried she might have had a heart attack or a stroke."

"She's fine," Jessie assured him, moved by his concern for the elderly woman who could have killed him had he stepped out of the vehicle before she'd slammed hers into Reverse. "You're the one who's been hurt."

He lifted a hand toward his face. "Just some burns from the air bag," he said, dismissing his injuries. "It's nothing."

"The chemical burned your eyes, too," she reminded him. "You can barely see right now."

"And Doc Malewitz put some drops in to treat them." He squinted at her, grimaced and added, "I can see better already."

"Close your eyes," she directed him, with a smile at his stubborn male pride. "Let them rest."

He expelled a ragged breath. "How come you keep getting the duty of driving me home?"

"I'm low man on the totem pole." She hoped like hell that was all it was. That the doctor and his wife were just too busy to drive patients home. She hoped she had just imagined the look that had passed between the sweet married couple and that they weren't trying to match her and the sheriff.

Maybe that was their contingency plan in case who-ever eventually took over their practice didn't keep her on as the medical secretary. Since she might lose her job, did they intend to find her a husband to support her? They had finally had that talk with her—the one she'd feared was coming for a while, because she'd seen the reluctance and guilt in their eyes. As soon as they found someone to take over their practice, they were going to retire to a warmer climate.

She sighed now and pushed aside her sense of aban-donment. It wasn't like eight years ago when her parents had retired on her and moved back to Germany when Jessie had needed them most—when she'd been preg-nant, scared and alone. It wasn't like that now because she had Tommy; she wasn't alone. And in a year, she'd have her nursing degree.

"I could have called Eleanor or one of the deputies to drive me home," he said.

"But you didn't," she remarked. "Last time or this time. Why not?"

He sighed. "I don't know. I guess I've wanted to spend some time with you."

Her heart raced then slowed with dread as she realized what he meant. "You're still working on keeping that promise to my son. You want me to tell you about his dad."

"I'd rather you told *him*."

"I will," she said, "when he's old enough to understand." Her breath shortened as a familiar panic returned. She knew she wouldn't be able to put it off much longer.

"I'm old enough," Chance pointed out. "Tell me. Let me help you."

"I don't need your help," she insisted. "Tommy's my son. I can handle this on my own. I don't need the local sheriff involved in my personal life."

"I don't want to get involved," Chance insisted, "...with you." The *especially* was unsaid but embarrassingly obvious from his tone.

She flinched even though she had already guessed he wasn't really attracted to her. But he kept looking at her. Even now when he was supposed to be resting his eyes, he studied her face. And not just her face. His gaze skimmed down her body, as well. As a secretary, she didn't have to wear a uniform to work. Since Forest Glen was pretty laid-back, she didn't have to dress up, either. She wore dark jeans and a green sweater in a thin fabric that clung to her breasts.

Her skin tingled in reaction to that intense stare of his. "Then maybe you should have had Eleanor drive you home." For both their sakes.

"Yeah, I should have," he agreed with embarrassing haste. "But I wanted to talk to you. About Tommy."

She tightened her rein on her temper. He'd just been hurt, so she was not going to get mad at him. Calmly but firmly, she said, "I am not going to tell you about his father."

"I want to talk about Tommy," he repeated. "I meant what I said the other day in the sporting goods store. I'd be happy to spend some time with him."

With her son, but not her.

"You think he'd be happy with just any old guy?" she asked.

"I'm not old," he said, his voice a little sharp as if he'd taken offense.

She spared a glance from the road to his handsome, albeit battered, face and sniffed in reluctant agreement.

"And he doesn't want to play catch with a girl," he reminded her, his mouth curving into a teasing grin. "I went ahead and bought that baseball glove."

"I appreciate your offer," she said honestly. Her son could use a man in his life for however long Chance Drayton stuck it out in Forest Glen. "I'll ask Tommy."

"He's talking to you?"

She smiled with pride. "He's too sweet-natured to stay mad at me."

"What about me?" Chance asked.

Her son's opinion of him mattered to the ex-Marine. Jessie's breath slipped out in a soft gasp. The man was nearly too good to be true.

"Show him your scars," she said. She'd overheard him and Christopher discussing how the former soldier must have several of them.

"I don't have any scars," he said, then grimaced as he leaned across the console and glanced at his face in the rearview mirror. "Well, not from Afghanistan."

"That's good—given what you must have gone through," she said with sympathy and curiosity.

"You don't want to talk about your past. I don't want to talk about mine."

"I understand." But she didn't. Not really. She couldn't imagine what he must have experienced. "Tommy might not be as understanding," she warned him. "Boys like hearing war stories."

He sighed. "Then I'm going to have to give him the same line you do—that he's too young to hear any of my war stories."

"I'm sorry," she said and lifted one hand from the wheel to reach across to him. Because his arm was wounded, scraped and burned from the air bag, she touched his leg instead. The muscles of his thigh tensed beneath her fingers, and she jerked her hand back. "I'm sorry," she said again.

His breath shuddered out. "Jessie…"

Her hands shaking, she steered the car into his driveway and put it into Park. Then she turned to him. She couldn't mistake the look in his eyes, the heat of desire.

He reached across the console now and slid his fingertips along her jaw, lifting her face to his. "You're not interested," she reminded him.

"I never said I wasn't interested," he clarified. "I just don't want to get involved with you."

"I don't want to get involved with you," she said, but she leaned closer and lifted her mouth to his.

As he started lowering his head, his lips just a breath

from hers, she jerked back. A man was watching them from the shadows of Chance's covered porch.

His fingers tensed along her jaw while his other hand slid into her hair. "Jessie—"

She shifted against the seat, pulling farther away. "You have company."

He turned then and peered out the windshield, first at the sports car with the Illinois plates and then at the man leaning over the teal-and-purple-painted railing near the front steps of the yellow farmhouse. "Damn."

"Who is he?" she asked. She didn't recognize the blond-haired stranger, but she already resented him a bit for what his presence had prevented: Chance's lips finally touching hers.

"My lawyer."

"Lawyer?" He wouldn't have had time since the accident to call the guy and summon him from another state, so he wasn't suing Mrs. Applegate. "Everything all right?"

"No," he said. With a weary sigh, he eased away from her and pushed open the passenger door. Then he stepped out and turned back to her. "Thanks for the ride home."

"You're not going to tell me anything else," she realized with disappointment.

He shook his head.

Even though they hadn't kissed, her lips tingled from how close he'd been, his breath whispering across her skin—promising sweet passion. But she pushed aside her regret at the lost moment and summoned her common sense. Until she and Chance were ready to share their secrets, they sure as hell weren't ready to share any kisses.

Chapter Six

"What the hell happened to you?" Trenton Sanders asked as Chance grimaced as he climbed the stairs to the porch, his sore ribs protesting every movement.

He ignored his friend's question and asked one of his own. "What are you doing here?"

When Chance had decided to move to Forest Glen, Trenton had sworn—with a dramatic shudder—that nothing would get him out to the *boonies* to visit—not even if the water supply turned into crude and the gravel gold.

"I've got news," the lawyer replied. Apparently he'd come straight from his office with it because he still wore one of his trademark tailored suits in a dark gray. He hadn't even loosened his tie despite the long drive up from Chicago.

"It better be good news." Or Chance might have to hurt him for interrupting what had promised to be a passionate kiss given the way Jessie had leaned into him, her eyes wide and dark with desire. He glanced toward the driveway as Jessie backed her small SUV onto the street.

Trenton followed his gaze. "Who's the hot redhead?"

He turned back to Chance and narrowed his eyes. "Did she do that to your face?"

Chance touched his jaw, wincing since the skin was still tender and raw from the airbag. Maybe Trenton had done him a favor. Considering the way Jessie kept Tommy from knowing anything about his dad, she was the last woman—next to his ex—that Chance should be kissing.

"You found a wild one, huh?" Trenton teased, his slick lawyer facade stripped back to the kid who had pitched to Chance on their winning team back in high school.

"What are you doing here?" Chance asked again, ignoring his old friend's inappropriate question. "You could have just called and told me what's going on."

Trenton goaded him with a grin. "But then I wouldn't have been able to see your face—ugly as it is—when I gave you the news."

Chance's heart skipped a beat. Had Robyn finally stopped stalling? Had a court date been set at last? "So tell me," he demanded. "What's going on?"

"I got you a visit with your son."

"What?" His eyes stung, and he wanted to blame it on the gas that had escaped the air bag. But he was too overwhelmed to bother lying to himself. After all this time, was it possible that he'd be seeing his boy again? "When?"

"His spring break from school," Trenton replied. "Middle of April."

Chance's breath caught; it was only a couple of weeks away. "Oh, my God. How'd you manage that?"

Trenton's brown eyes twinkled slightly. "What makes you think I had anything to do with it?"

Because Trenton Sanders earned his high fees with a reputation as the lawyer who had never lost a case. "Because you probably did."

"I can't claim any credit for this one," Trenton insisted. "Not without getting disbarred. But really, Matthew's the one who talked to his mom."

"You talked to him," Chance said—with gratitude and jealousy. He hadn't spoken with his own son, in person or on the phone, since Robyn had refused him visitation. She'd moved to an unlisted address with no landline. The only contact information Chance had for her was her cell phone, which she let go to voice mail whenever he tried to call. That was why he'd hired Trenton.

"That conversation never happened," his friend insisted. "The important one is the one he had with his mother when he told her he wants to spend his spring break from school with his father."

"And Robyn agreed?"

Trenton sighed. "Not easily. And only to this one visit. She won't agree to regular visitation."

"That's why we have to take her to court," Chance said. He hadn't wanted to, but she'd left him no choice since she wouldn't even speak to him. "I want more than one week with my son."

"This is a great opportunity to prove to Robyn and to the judge that you're ready for Matthew," Trenton pointed out. "That you have room in your house and your life for him."

"Of course I do." Everything he'd done since coming back from Afghanistan had been for Matthew. "This house—this town—is perfect for raising a child."

"But your future here isn't secure, according to

Robyn's lawyer. That's what they're going to argue when we go before the judge."

"I own this house free and clear." he reminded the man who'd helped him negotiate probate. "I inherited it."

"But the job is only interim," Trenton said with a sigh. "The mayor and city council hired you on a trial basis only."

And since Chance had taken the mayor's mother's driver's license that afternoon, that trial was probably over. The mayor had showed up at the accident scene, and he had been furious to find out that Chance had impounded her car and suspended her license. "If they don't elect me in the fall, I can apply for a job with the state police."

"You want to wait until fall to go before the judge?" Trenton asked.

"Of course not." He'd already been denied a relationship with his child for too long.

"Then you'll need to be able to prove that your future in Forest Glen is secure. Now."

"I'll prove it," he promised, grateful that he hadn't kissed Jessie Phillips. He needed to focus on building a life for his son—not letting a woman disrupt his own life.

JESSIE SLIPPED into the back of the meeting hall, noticed her cousin waving and headed over to the vacant chair next to Belinda. "Since when do you attend town council meetings?" she asked.

"Since the yummy new sheriff's on the agenda," Belinda replied with a wink.

Jessie glanced around the crowded room and

wondered how many other women, single and married, were there just to ogle the sexy young sheriff, too. She caught several people staring back at her. Her boss, Dr. Malewitz, and his wife Ruth waved. And Eleanor, the sheriff's secretary and dispatcher, turned around from the chair in front of Jessie and smiled.

Did everyone think that was why she was there—because she had a thing for the new sheriff? But she always attended the council meetings; she liked knowing what was going on in her community. After spending her childhood moving from one military base to another, she liked being a permanent part of a community.

She breathed a sigh of relief as the mayor, from the table at the front of the dark paneled room, called the meeting to order. Mr. Applegate droned on about approving last month's minutes and covered some new business before turning the floor over to the sheriff.

Chance moved to the podium at the front of the room and cleared his throat. He glanced around the crowd, his gaze stopping on Jessie. Her pulse quickened, and heat rushed to her face as other people noticed him looking at her. Then he spoke. "I want to tell everyone how much I'm enjoying my job as sheriff, so much that I would like to be included on the ballot for the election this fall."

Applause rang out.

But the mayor's mouth gaped open in shock at the announcement, and he waved everyone to silence. "Are you sure about this, Drayton?" the bald-headed, portly man asked. "You've had an eventful couple of months—at least by Forest Glen standards."

"Not by my standards," Chance said with a reassuring grin.

"Really?" the older man challenged him. "You've had to make two trips to the doctor's office. Maybe this job is a little more than you can handle."

Even from a few rows back, Jessie noticed how Chance clenched his jaw. Being a Marine might have prepared him for law enforcement but not for small-town politics. "I spent years on the police force in Chicago, and I did two tours in Afghanistan," he reminded his interim boss.

"Yes, but you had an entire force to back you up in Chicago, and a platoon in Afghanistan," Mayor Applegate pointed out. "Here, you can't even handle a traffic stop without your vehicle having to be towed."

"Now, you all know that I'm the one who caused that accident," someone spoke up, but her voice was just a weak quaver from the front of the room.

Jessie arched her neck, trying to peer over other heads to see Mrs. Applegate. Even standing, the elderly woman was tiny.

"And I'm awfully sorry about that," she continued. "I could have seriously injured this young man. Or as he pointed out when he took my driver's license, I could have hurt someone else—" Then her voice grew stronger as she turned on her son. "Archie, you should have had the balls to take away my license when I first started having these accidents. You should have cared enough to get me off the road."

The mayor audibly gulped. "Mother, I thought you didn't want to lose your independence."

"It wasn't about me," she snapped at her son. "You didn't want me to become dependent on you. You resent having to drive me to my appointments since the sheriff took my license. And it's only been a week."

"Mother—"

"This young man is the best thing to have happened to this damn town in a long while," she continued, undeterred. "He will truly protect and serve us."

"Hear, hear." Mrs. Wilson seconded her comments.

The room erupted into applause again. There was no doubt that Chance would win the election. It was Mrs. Applegate's endorsement that had elected her son as mayor. The realization that Drayton might become a permanent part of Forest Glen had Jessie fighting for air. With a nod at her cousin, she slipped from her chair and snuck out of the crowded room.

Tommy waited in the beautiful park outside the community building. Under the supervision of the school crossing guard, he played on the equipment with several other kids whose parents were also attending the meeting. As she crossed the lush, spring grass to where he climbed over the metal cage of the jungle gym, she braced herself for a battle to get him to leave. But he rushed up to her right away.

He wasn't looking at her, though. Instead he was looking at the man who'd followed her out. "Hi, Sheriff," he said, his voice soft with embarrassment. "I'm sorry I was such a jerk last Saturday at Smith's."

"You weren't a jerk," Chance assured him, crouching to his level. "I'm the one who was a jerk. I shouldn't have made you a promise until I talked to your mom."

Tommy nodded in acceptance. But Jessie felt his disappointment in a rush of guilt that overwhelmed her. She wouldn't be able to put off the inevitable much longer. If only she could lie to him without feeling even guiltier than she did now...

"I actually need to ask you a favor," Chance said.

Her son's bright eyes widened in surprise. "You do?"

"I need your help."

"With what?"

"My son is going to be coming to stay with me during his spring break."

"You have a child?" Jessie said, beating Tommy to the question.

Chance clenched that strong jaw again and nodded. "He's just a couple of years older than Tommy here. I haven't seen him in a while, so I don't know what he likes. I don't have any idea what kids like nowadays, but I need to get his room ready for him. Will you help me?"

Tommy shrugged. "Sure. But Mom's the one who painted my room and stuff."

"I'd be happy to help you," Jessie found herself offering, if only because she wanted to know the story that darkened Chance's eyes with pain.

"I know, I know!" Tommy exclaimed, his voice ringing with excitement now.

Chance chuckled. "What do you know?"

She wondered if he'd be surprised by her son's intelligence, or if he'd already picked up on that for himself despite his lack of familiarity with kids. Even his own.

"You should build him a tree house," Tommy said as if he'd figured out the answer to some complex problem, which he regularly did to the astonishment of the teachers who struggled to keep him challenged and engaged in school.

Jessie smiled. Her little boy might surprise other people, but she knew him well. "Really? A tree house?

What makes you think the sheriff's son would like that?"

"'Cause every boy wants a tree house," he replied with a snort of disgust at her ignorance.

Chance nodded, as if Tommy had offered him very sage advice. "You're right. I always wanted a tree house when I was a kid. But I lived in a city like Matthew and his mom, so I couldn't have one."

"So you gotta do it," Tommy said with absolute resolution. "For both of you."

Jessie suspected he'd figured there was something in this tree house suggestion for him, too.

"Can you help me build it?" Chance asked.

Tommy jerked his red head up and down in a vigorous nod. "Yeah! We'll make it so cool that he won't want to go back to the stupid city."

Chance audibly caught his breath, and Jessie noted the wistful longing in his eyes.

"I'm going to need help with some other things, too," he said. "Remember I told you I'm rusty at playing catch. Well, it's not just catch. I haven't played any other games in a long time."

"I'll teach you," Tommy offered.

The sheriff held out his hand, and the two males sealed their agreement with a firm shake. Then Tommy pulled away with a giggle. "I have to go tell Christopher that I'm gonna be building a tree house."

"Hey, we need to get home," Jessie called after her son, but he was already running back to his friend.

"Is that okay?" Chance asked. "Or should I have run it past you first?"

She turned toward him with a sigh. "That might have

been a good idea, especially after the last time you made an arrangement with my son."

"Yeah, I wasn't thinking."

"You're too excited," she said, noticing how his eyes glittered just like Tommy's. "You haven't seen your son in a while?"

"Not since I deployed last time," he said, his voice rough with frustration. "My ex filed for full custody because I volunteered for a second deployment after my first."

"Full custody," she murmured, her stomach churning at the thought. Chance should understand more than anyone else why she wasn't willing to take the risk of revealing Tommy's paternity.

"Now I'm doing the same."

"What?" she asked, shocked at the bitterness and resentment in his deep voice.

"I'm suing her for full custody."

She released a sigh of regret. He wouldn't understand, especially since he'd just given her another reason not to contact Tommy's father—the fear that he might react as vengefully as Chance had. "So you want to take him away from his mother, uproot him from his school and his friends and move him here to Forest Glen?"

"You don't understand the situation," he said, his jaw tense again.

Jessie laughed at his hypocrisy. "That sounds familiar."

"I want what's best for my son," he insisted.

"Me, too."

He nodded, as if he'd finally accepted her right to keep Tommy's paternity secret. "Matthew will love it here," he said, "like I did when I used to come stay with my grandma. It's a great place to raise a kid." He looked at her inquisitively. "Isn't that why you stay?"

She'd always figured that she was here because she didn't have anywhere else to go. But even if she did, she wouldn't leave. Forest Glen was the home she'd always wanted. "It's a great town," she agreed. "So you're staying?"

"For now."

"You'll win the election this fall," she assured him, as if he could have had any doubts after the reaction to his announcement to run.

"It's not the election I'm worried about."

"The custody case," she said again, her stomach churning with her own fears regarding such a battle.

"I thought about it before I filed," he said. "I really feel that I can give him much more than I'd be taking away from him."

"You think you can replace his mother?" she asked, horrified.

"No. But I think I can be as good a parent, if not better. I'll have more time to spend with him here than Robyn ever has."

And he thought he'd be able to make up for the time he'd been away from his son. She understood. She didn't agree with what he was doing, but she understood. If only he could really do the same with her...

"So if you don't win full custody, you won't stay here?" she asked.

His broad shoulders lifted in a jerky shrug. "I don't know what I'll do."

The hint of vulnerability in his words had Jessie reaching out to him. Her fingers skimmed across the back of his hand. Her touch was the only support she could offer him. He turned his hand over. His fingers brushed across hers, then entwined. He squeezed.

Tommy glanced up from his conversation with Christopher and stared at their joined hands. Jessie tugged her hand free of Chance's. No doubt Tommy wasn't the only one who'd noticed as the crowd spilled from the meeting hall behind them.

"You don't know what you've done," she murmured.

"What do you mean?" he asked with a slight grin.

She sighed and tilted her head in the direction of their audience. "You followed me out of there, right?"

"Yes. I intended to ask you if you would mind my talking to Tommy and enlisting his help, but then he ran up."

"You followed me out in front of everyone?"

He nodded again and then grimaced as realization dawned. "Oh."

"Yeah," she said. "People were already gossiping about us, and now..."

"Do you care?"

"No," she admitted, except it might encourage her boss's matchmaking and increase her cousin's teasing. "I stopped caring what people thought about me a long time ago."

"Let me guess...eight years ago?"

"Yes."

"So you'll still help me get my house ready for Matthew?"

"Tommy's helping you." And she was okay with that; Tommy could use a strong male role model.

"He doesn't paint," Chance reminded her. "And neither do I."

She had offered to help, but with her skin tingling

from just the brief touch of his hand, she debated the wisdom of that decision. It might be good for Tommy to have a man in his life, but she wasn't so sure about herself. Actually, she wasn't so sure about this man... not after learning that he was doing to his ex what she feared most. He was taking away her son.

Chapter Seven

"Wow," Chance murmured as he stared down at the paper Tommy Phillips had unfurled across the table in the kitchen of the old farmhouse. He'd expected a crude crayon drawing when the kid had announced he'd drawn up the plans for the tree house. But these sketches were detailed and realistic and looked nearly professional.

He glanced over the boy's head to meet Jessie's gaze where she leaned against the white cabinets. "I thought you were going to nursing school, not architecture."

"I am," she said, her lips curving into a slight smile. "He did it himself."

Chance turned to Tommy then. "You did this on your own?"

The redhead bobbed. "Yeah. I looked up some tree house plans online and made some 'justments. I figured you'd wanna spend some time up there, too, so it had to be big enough for you." The kid's small finger pointed out the support beams he'd penciled in. "That's why I put in these, to hold everything up."

"Wow," Chance said again. The kid really was bright. "This is amazing. I couldn't have done better myself."

Tommy's face flushed nearly as red as his freckles, but he beamed with pride and pleasure at Chance's compliment. Then the kid wadded up the plans, crumpled them under his arm, and jerked open the back door of the kitchen. "What tree?" he asked as he rushed out into the yard.

Jessie moved to follow her son, but Chance caught her, wrapping his fingers lightly around her wrist. She shivered, but it couldn't have been from cold. Afternoon sunshine warmed the yard and the house. She lifted her gaze to his, her green eyes dilating as he leaned closer. He was tempted to steal that kiss his friend had interrupted a week ago, but Tommy turned around and called back to them.

"You two coming?" he asked, his voice high with excitement and impatience.

Chance nodded. "In a minute."

"I'm sorry we just dropped in," Jessie said, tugging her wrist free of his grasp. "If you're in the middle of something…"

He shook his head. "No. I'm glad you came by so soon. But when I asked you for help the other day, I didn't expect…"

Her lips curved into a slight smile. "No one does. Tommy's my little genius."

"He is," Chance agreed. "How can you not think that a kid that smart would be able to understand whatever your story is about his father?"

Jessie's eyes narrowed, and her lips tightened into that stubborn line. "My story? Whatever I tell Tommy will be the truth."

"What is it, Jessie?" he asked. He wanted to know for more than Tommy's sake now. He wanted to know for his own.

She dragged in an audible breath as if bracing herself.

"I didn't come over here for you to interrogate me again," she said, and gestured toward her faded jeans and paint-stained sweatshirt. "Tommy and I came to help you get ready for your son's visit."

Visit? While his heart beat faster in anticipation of finally seeing his boy again, a week wasn't good enough. He needed more time than that with his son. "I do appreciate—"

"Then let's call a truce," she suggested. "I don't agree with you going for full custody of your son—"

"You don't understand," he interrupted defensively, even as guilt nagged at him.

"And you don't understand why I want to wait to tell Tommy about his father," she said. "So let's just accept that about each other."

"We could try," he suggested. Maybe if he could convince her he was doing the right thing, he could rid himself of his niggling doubts and guilt.

She shook her head. "For now, since you have such a short time to get ready for your son's visit, I think we should just agree to disagree. No more promises or judgments."

"So a truce," he said, repeating her offer.

She nodded. "We won't talk about our reasons for being single parents."

"For now," he agreed. But he wanted to have that talk with her someday, wanted to understand her reasons and her to understand his. He extended his hand.

She slid her palm against his, her fingers trembling slightly. Her skin was silky and warm, and that warmth spread up his arm. He wanted to tug her closer and finally take that kiss he'd been denied too long.

"Mom! Sheriff!" Tommy shouted. "C'mon!"

Jessie pulled free and rushed out to join her son in the yard. More slowly, his heart pounding hard, Chance followed her.

"That tree," Tommy said, pointing to the tallest oak. "That's it!"

With its thick branches, it was the best choice for the tree house. Chance settled his hand onto the boy's thin shoulder. "Yeah, that's the tree."

"Then we better get building," Tommy said. "Where are your tools?"

Chance steered him over to the pile of lumber he'd bought. And he lifted off the small tool apron he'd picked up for the boy. "This is for you."

Tommy grinned and wrapped the belt around his waist. "This is cool."

Chance glanced over at Jessie, who was still staring up at the tree. He left Tommy at the pile of lumber and walked back over to her. "Is this all right?" he asked.

"I'm not sure I want Tommy that high up in the tree," she admitted, her voice quavering slightly. "I don't want him getting hurt."

"I'll make sure he doesn't," Chance assured her.

She stared up at him now, as fearfully as she had at the tree. "I thought you weren't going to make any more promises you might not be able to keep."

And he knew that she wasn't just talking about Tommy getting physically hurt. She was talking about him getting too attached to Chance and Chance having to leave if he lost his custody battle. "You're right," he agreed. "I can't make any more promises."

To Tommy or to his mother.

"SO DO YOU THINK that tree's big enough?" Christopher asked.

Tommy stepped back and eyed the pine tree the same way Chance had sized up the oak in his backyard. The sheriff's backyard was a lot bigger and had way more older trees than Tommy and his mom's puny yard. He shook his head. "Nah. It's not as tall as the one Chance and me built his tree house in."

"Chance?"

"The sheriff," he said then drew in a breath that puffed out his chest. "He told me to call him Chance."

"You and your mom been spending a lot of time with him," Christopher said, and he was looking at Tommy like Tommy had looked at that tree, sizing him up. Christopher was a year older than him and pretty smart.

"Yeah. Mom's been painting inside the house for him. She's good at that dec'rating stuff." 'Course she'd asked his opinion, and Tommy had been sure to tell her that ten was too old for trains or stuffed animals or any other baby stuff. She'd promised to redo his room after she finished at the sheriff's house. "Matthew's gonna love what she did over there."

Like the yard, the house was bigger than theirs, too, with lots of big rooms and a scary attic and basement. Cool places for hide and seek.

"Who's Matthew?" Christopher asked.

"I told you," he said with an impatient sigh. Maybe Christopher wasn't as smart as Tommy had thought. It would be cool to hang out with someone even older than Christopher and more grown up, like Matthew. "He's the sheriff's son."

"The sheriff's married?" Christopher asked.

Tommy sighed again, disgusted that his friend couldn't keep up with him. But then most kids couldn't. That was why he usually hung out with older kids. Would Matt want to hang out with him? "Not all moms and dads are married like yours, you know."

"Yeah, yeah, I know…"

"Chance is divorced from Matthew's mom. She's finally letting him come visit, so Chance has had me and Mom helping him get ready." Tommy rolled his shoulder, which was a little sore from all the catch he'd played. Chance had told Tommy that he was really good at throwing, that he'd probably be a pitcher in the big leagues some day. He'd felt super proud.

"So when's he coming?" Christopher asked.

"Spring break. It's the same as ours."

"Next week, too?"

"Three days from today." He and Chance had been marking the days off on the calendar they'd put up in the tree house.

"Me and my folks are going to Disney World," Christopher said, as if Tommy didn't already know, as if the kid hadn't been telling everyone every day.

Tommy had been jealous, before, that his friend was going to get to go on all those rides. But now he didn't care. He was going to have fun, too, this break—with Chance and Matthew and his mom. "That's cool," he said.

"Yeah. It's cool you're helping out the sheriff," Christopher said. "Too bad he wasn't your dad, huh?"

Tommy's heart skipped a beat. "Yeah…but he's not."

"You know somebody doesn't have to be your dad to be your dad."

Tommy wrinkled his forehead in confusion. "Huh?"

"Somebody can become your dad even if you don't have the same bio...biolog...blood."

"What do you mean?"

"Like me," Christopher said. "I'm adopted."

"What?" Shock froze Tommy in place. Then he shook his head at his friend's fib. "Yeah, right, you look just like your dad."

Christopher laughed. "Everybody says that. And it's cool. But he adopted me. Still, he's my dad."

"So you don't know your real dad, either?" Tommy asked.

His friend shook his head, messing up his sandy brown curls. "Nope. And I don't care. I'd rather be with somebody who wants me than someone who doesn't."

Tommy's heart hurt, as if it were getting squeezed. "Yeah, you're right. My dad doesn't want anything to do with me so I don't want anything to do with him!"

A loud gasp brought his attention round to the little deck at the back of his house. His mom leaned on the railing, and from the surprised look on her face, she must have heard what he said.

But she turned to his friend instead. "Christopher, your mother called. She wants you home for dinner."

Probably wanting out of the weird situation, his friend waved goodbye and headed around the house to the front gate.

"Is our dinner ready?" Tommy asked.

"Yes," his mom replied. "But we need to talk first."

"'Bout what?" he asked, even though he knew. She'd definitely heard him. Her face was all serious-looking.

"I didn't know you thought that," she said, her eyes shiny as if she was about to cry.

Tommy shrugged. "I get it. My dad's not around because he doesn't want to be. He doesn't want to be a dad." Not like Chance did. Chance couldn't wait to see his son, to hang out with him. He wished his dad was like that. He wished his dad was Chance.

"I'm sorry, honey," his mother said, her voice all soft and shaky.

Tears stung his eyes, but he blinked them back. He was not going to be a baby. "It's okay…"

"No, it's not," she said. "Your dad doesn't know about you. I never told him."

JESSIE WISHED the words back the minute she uttered them. But she couldn't let Tommy believe that he'd been rejected. Keith had rejected her, not their son. Why had it never occurred to her that Tommy might believe that his father knew about him but wanted nothing to do with him?

And maybe it was true; maybe Keith wouldn't want anything to do with him even if he was aware that he had a son.

"Tommy, I'm so sorry," she said, the words a whisper from the emotion choking her.

His eyes welling with tears, he shook his head. "You're not sorry!"

"Yes, I am," she insisted. Guilt and regret overwhelmed her. "I should have told him about you. He would love you." Even if he wasn't eager to be a father, Keith wouldn't reject Tommy; he wouldn't be able to resist their son. No one could. "Everybody who knows you loves you."

"You don't!" he shouted, his face flushing dark with anger. "You don't love me!"

"Yes, I do," she said. And that was why she'd been so scared of losing him. "I love you more than anyone else in this world."

"If you loved me, you'd tell me the truth instead of treating me like a dumb baby," he argued. "I'm not a baby!"

Not anymore. Her little boy had grown up when she wasn't looking. His teachers all praised his intelligence and his maturity. Maybe because it was just the two of them, he'd grown up faster than he should have and acted far older than his eight years. He was mature enough to know the truth of what she'd done.

"Tommy, I know that you're not a baby," she agreed, "so I can tell you now. I'll tell you everything you want to know."

He shook his head. "I don't want to talk to you. Not anymore. Not ever again! I hate you!"

Jessie wasn't too crazy about herself at the moment, but she couldn't condone his speaking to her that way. "Tommy..." She reached for him, trying to close her hands over his shaking shoulders.

But he jerked away from her, as if he couldn't bear for her to touch him. "I hate you," he said again, his voice colder than she'd ever heard it.

And there was no mistaking the look in his eyes. At this moment, he meant what he said. Then he turned and ran in the direction his friend had gone, around the house and toward the gate at the front.

She restrained herself from chasing after him. After what she'd just revealed, she understood that he needed some time alone to calm down. And she needed a moment to dash away her tears and compose herself.

He didn't mean it. Her loving, sweet son couldn't really hate her, not like she hated herself right now. Her legs shaking, she walked back into the house where their dinner cooled on the kitchen table. She'd made his favorite: lasagna with extra cheese and a salad he claimed he didn't like but then always ate seconds. She picked up the cordless phone and dialed the Johnsons' number, then cradled the receiver between her ear and her shoulder as she put the food away in plastic containers. Tommy would be hungry when he came home but maybe too tired from his emotional outburst to eat.

The Johnsons' phone kept ringing before going to voice mail. They had a no answering phones during dinner rule; Tommy had told her about all their family rules. She needed to take notes herself since she hadn't done much right with her parenting. After the beep, she said, "This is Jessie. Please call me back and let me know that Tommy's at your house. He's really mad at me now, so if you wouldn't mind keeping him for the night, I'd appreciate it. I'll be over in a bit with his pajamas, toothbrush and clothes for school tomorrow. Then I'll explain what's going on."

Since tomorrow was Friday, they'd probably be happy to have Tommy. After putting away the food, she headed upstairs to pack his overnight bag. In the morning, after he'd calmed down, she would talk to him. She'd tell him everything and hope that he wouldn't really hate her.

CHANCE LEANED against the jamb of Matthew's new bedroom. He crossed his arms over his chest and felt his heart thump hard and fast. Would the room be okay with Matthew? Would he like it enough to want to stay the entire week?

He had no idea anymore what his boy liked. Kids grew up so fast, changed so much in just a little while. And it had been over a year since he'd seen Matthew. Thanks to Tommy's help, though, Chance had learned what Matthew probably wouldn't like, what he'd be too old for. So they'd decided on skateboards and snowboards and surfboards for his room. They'd found wall clings and complemented the bright colors of the boards with dark-colored paint.

Jessie had worked hard to make the room vibrant and cool. Closing his eyes, he remembered the smear of navy blue on her nose and along her cheek. And the shimmery silver paint sprinkled through her red hair. Disheveled and slightly flushed from her exertion, she'd been even more beautiful to him.

She hadn't had to help him. The way he'd treated her since Tommy had stepped into his office, she shouldn't have helped him. But her heart was too soft, her spirit too generous to refuse him assistance. He uttered a ragged sigh and ran his palm over his face. Without her and Tommy, he wouldn't have had a clue about how to get ready for his son's visit. Maybe Robyn was right about him. Maybe he wasn't cut out to be a father.

But then he remembered Tommy's smiling face as the little boy had swung the hammer against the nail Chance had held for him. He grimaced and glanced down at his black thumbnail. *That* hadn't been the nail Tommy was supposed to hammer into the wood.

"Mom can kiss it better," Tommy had offered.

Chance bet she could. And he'd come so close to kissing her over the past week and a half. But he'd held himself back every time he'd been tempted to lean in, to close the distance between her lips and his. He'd gotten so close a few times that he'd tasted the sweetness of her breath and had felt its warmth whisper across his skin. But he wanted to be a good father this time. He couldn't put anything—or anyone—before his son again.

His ringing cell phone startled him from his thoughts. Hoping it was Matthew, he pulled his cell from his pocket and glanced at the LCD screen. He didn't recognize the number but, as he'd learned, his job wasn't nine to five. Citizens of Forest Glen felt free to call him at any time, day or night. Glancing at the darkened windows, he noted that night had fallen. He answered the phone, "Sheriff Drayton."

"Chance, I can't find him." Sobs cracked the familiar voice. "I—I can't find him anywhere."

"Jessie?" It wasn't her number on the ID. Over the past several days that she and Tommy had been helping him, she'd called him enough times that he'd memorized her number. Hell, if she'd only called once he would have memorized it. "What's wrong?"

"Tommy's gone."

"Where are you?" he asked.

"At my cousin's. I checked the Johnsons'. I thought he went over there after he ran away from me."

"He ran away from you?" Chance swallowed a groan, remembering when Tommy had run off at the store—angry over his dad. "I thought he'd dropped that idea…"

"Only because he believed his father wants nothing to do with him," Jessie said, "and I couldn't let him think that he'd been rejected. But once I admitted I'd never told his dad about him, he got so mad that he took off."

Chance sucked in a breath even though he wasn't really surprised. He'd suspected that was why she'd listed Tommy's father as unknown, because she hadn't told the guy she was pregnant.

"I thought he went down to the Johnsons'," she continued, "but he wasn't there. And he's not at Belinda's. I checked some of his other friends' houses." Her voice cracked again, choked with sobs and fear. "I don't know where else to look."

Chance narrowed his eyes as he stared out that darkened window into the backyard. The glimmers of light he'd thought were fireflies might be something else entirely. "I think I know where he is." He hurried down the curved stairwell and out the back door of the kitchen. The light he'd glimpsed from inside spilled from the tree house onto the yard beneath the oak. The way it flickered, it had to be coming from the old lantern.

How had the little boy gotten it lit? But then, this was Tommy; there probably wasn't much the kid couldn't figure out, except why his mother had done what she had. He wasn't the only one who struggled to understand. That, more than anything else, had held Chance back from kissing her. How could he get involved with a woman who'd done exactly as his ex had? Kept a child from his father...

"Is he with you?" Jessie asked, her voice quavering through the phone.

"He's here...in the tree house," he whispered.

"I'll be right over."

"Give us a little bit of time. Let me talk to him first." Maybe he was prying again, poking his nose in where it didn't belong. Guess that meant he had truly become a citizen of Forest Glen. But over the past several days, he'd formed a relationship with the boy—a closer one than he had with his own son right now.

Jessie released a shaky breath that rattled over the phone. "Okay."

And he knew what that concession meant. She'd trusted him with what mattered most to her: her son. He couldn't let her down now. He clicked off his cell and shoved it back in his pocket, then headed closer to the tree house. He reached for the rope ladder hanging from the trap door, and before he'd even poked his head through the hole, he heard the sniffles and shaky breaths. When Chance cleared the floor, Tommy whirled away from him and lifted his fists to his face, dashing away tears.

"Go away," the boy mumbled around the sobs shaking his shoulders. "I just wanna be alone."

Chance shifted around in the small room so that he sat on the edge of the opening, dangling his legs through the hole. And maybe Tommy thought Chance had taken him at his word because he lifted his head. Then he vaulted himself into Chance's arms. Chance caught him close, so he wouldn't slip through the trap door. And because the kid obviously needed a hug.

"Don't go!" Tommy beseeched him, his voice soft and quivery, laying bare his vulnerability and loneliness. He had to feel as if the one person he'd always counted on—the only constant in his young life—had betrayed him.

Chance's heart ached with the child's pain. He patted the boy's back. "I'm not going anywhere. We can just sit here or we can talk. Whatever you want."

"I want to stay here—with you," Tommy said. "I don't want to go home."

"Your mother loves you." Chance had no doubt about that. He had watched them interact; Jessie's beautiful face glowed with love every time she looked at her son. And she constantly touched the boy, squeezing his shoulder, kissing his forehead and hugging him. "You are her whole world."

Tommy sniffled louder, and his tears dampened the front of Chance's shirt. "I told her I hated her." And maybe he was more upset about that than what he'd learned.

"She knows you didn't mean it," Chance assured the distraught boy.

Tommy pulled back and stared up at him, his eyes wide and wet. "I was so mad I felt like I meant it. How could she...how could she...?" His voice cracked on another sob, this one of frustration.

"I'm sure your mom has her reasons for not telling your dad about you," he said. "You just have to trust her."

Mentally he called himself a hypocrite. He could tell her son to trust her, but he couldn't quite trust her himself. Too much of what she'd done, of the way she treated Tommy, reminded him of Robyn. It was good that Chance had never kissed Jessie Phillips or he might have formed a deeper attachment to her than he already had. And then he'd probably wind up feeling as betrayed and heartbroken as her son.

Chapter Eight

The light from the hall shone across his face, his eyes closed as he lay sleeping in the top bunk in Chance's son's room. Jessie crept closer and extended her hand, running her fingertips across her son's cheek. The skin was damp yet from all the tears he'd shed—because of her.

Strong hands closed over her shoulders, and a muscular chest pressed against her back, offering support in his strength and comfort in his warmth. "Let him sleep," a deep voice persuaded her. "He's exhausted. He wore himself out."

Tears stung her eyes and she could only nod.

"He's fine here," Chance assured her. He turned her, his arm around her shoulders, and guided her back toward the open door of the bedroom and out into the wide hallway.

"This is the safest house in Forest Glen," she replied, "the sheriff's house." Tommy probably felt more protected here, with Chance, than he'd ever felt with her. After realizing she was a liar, would he ever trust her again? Had she completely destroyed their relationship?

Chance waggled his bruised thumb on her shoulder. "Not quite the safest. At least not for the sheriff."

She smiled, remembering how he'd fought to hide his grimace of pain from her son and insisted he was fine despite the twitching muscle along his tightly clenched jaw. "Tommy feels really bad about hitting you with the hammer."

"I know." Chance guided her farther down the hall, away from that open door, probably so they would not wake up the sleeping boy. The fact that they moved closer to the master bedroom was just a coincidence, she was certain. "He also feels really bad about what he said to you."

Her breath hitched. "That he hates me."

"He didn't mean it."

"The look on his face..." She shivered. "He's gotten mad at me before, but he's never looked at me like that. My little boy was gone."

"He's right there," Chance said, gesturing back toward his son's bedroom. "Drooling in his sleep."

She tried to smile but tears pooled in her eyes. She blinked them back and struggled to steady her breath. "He should hate me," Jessie said. "I hate myself. I've been so selfish."

"You're being too hard on yourself," he protested.

She shook her head as a smile freely curved her lips. "Now who's lying? You've been thinking all along— from the minute Tommy asked you to find his dad—that I was being selfish."

"I had no right to judge you without knowing what your situation is," he said. "This custody battle with Robyn had me unfairly jumping to conclusions about you."

"You think I'm like her," she said. She'd realized it the minute she'd learned about his son and that his ex-wife had sued him for full custody while he was in Afghanistan.

He chuckled. "You're nothing like Robyn."

From the way he'd said it, she had no idea if that was a good thing or a bad thing.

"So you never compared us?" she persisted.

He shook his head. "I can't claim that. I have compared what you've done to what she's doing to me."

"It's not the same," she insisted. "You were always there for Matthew."

"Except when I was deployed," he said with a sigh.

"Even when you were away, you were part of his life. You two always knew about each other. I never told Tommy's father about him."

"So they never had a relationship."

"Because I was too selfish to allow it." She bit her lip and shook her head, disgusted with herself. "I wanted to keep my little boy all to myself."

"You're scared," Chance said. "I've seen it in your eyes every time Tommy or I talked about finding his dad. Was that it, what held you back from telling this man that you were pregnant? You were afraid of him?"

"I was afraid of what he'd do," she admitted.

Chance reached for her again, his arms winding around her and offering comfort once more. And protection. "Was he abusive to you?"

"No, never," she replied with vehemence. Keith had always been a sweet boy, but she had no idea what kind of man he had become. "I'm afraid to find him now because I'm worried that he'll take my little boy away from me."

"And finding out I'm suing Robyn for full custody probably didn't calm your fears any."

She shook her head. "No, it didn't. But I think I was just looking for an excuse to keep Tommy away from his dad."

"Who is he?"

"Keith Howard—my high school sweetheart," she said. "He was a year ahead of me. He left for college before I confirmed I was pregnant, and I lied to him about the test results. I didn't want him coming home because he felt he had to. I wanted him to come home because he wanted to. You know."

Chance nodded. "I think I do," he said, as if he'd realized something about himself, as well. "So Keith didn't come home on his own?"

She shook her head, her eyes stinging as she remembered her old heartache. "Instead he sent me a Dear Jane letter dumping me."

"Ouch."

"And my pride was too hurt for me to admit that I'd lied and that I was actually pregnant. And every time I thought about finding him and telling him the truth, I'd take out that letter and read it again." She sighed. "I've taken it out quite a few times over the years." Keith hadn't loved her, so trapping him in a relationship he hadn't wanted wouldn't have been fair to him. But now, seeing Chance's misery over the separation from his son, she realized it hadn't been fair keeping Keith and Tommy apart.

Just because Keith had left her didn't mean he would do the same with his son. Would he reject him now? Her heart ached for Tommy's pain if he did.

"Thank you," Chance said, his deep blue gaze steady on her face.

Her skin heated under his scrutiny while she furrowed her brow in confusion. "What are you thanking me for?"

"For sharing your story with me."

She drew in a bracing breath. "I have a reason for doing that," she said, having made her decision when she'd been frantically searching for her son. "I want you to help me find him."

"Are you sure?"

She glanced back to that open bedroom door and swallowed hard, forcing down her doubts and fear. "Yes. I want you to keep that promise you made to Tommy. I want you to find his dad."

"What do you know about Keith Howard now? Have you kept in touch at all?"

"No. While he was away at college, I moved here to live with my aunt and my cousin."

"And you never told him where you moved," he surmised.

"No. After that Dear Jane letter, I didn't have any contact with him." And over the years, fear had replaced her wounded pride and bruised heart as the reason for not doing so.

"Do you know where he is?" Chance asked, and in full lawman mode, he fired more questions at her. "Did he move home after he finished college? And where is home? Where did you live before here?"

"For the end of my sophomore year and all of my junior year of high school, I lived in Fort Leonard Wood in Missouri," she said. She'd lost track of all the places she'd lived before then, traveling from base to base.

"Fort? You're from a military family?"

She nodded. "My father. He met my mother when he was stationed in Germany, and they moved back there before Tommy was born."

"So they don't see much of him?"

"Just in pictures. They've sent tickets for us to travel there, but…"

He didn't prod with anything but his steady, compassionate gaze, and those strong arms wrapped tight around her again.

So she answered his unspoken question. "I haven't quite gotten over them not being here for me when I needed them."

"They just left you?" He eased away from her and cupped her shoulders in his big palms.

"I could have gone with them," she admitted. "But moving out of the country when I was pregnant and had a year of high school left…"

"You'd already had enough on your plate." His hands squeezed before he released her.

"More than I could handle alone." She sighed. With him no longer touching her, she felt alone again, as if she had already come to depend on his comfort and strength. "Thank God for Aunt Sue and Belinda. I don't know what I would have done without their support."

"I don't think I've met your aunt." But Belinda had undoubtedly introduced herself.

"Aunt Sue moved away a couple of years ago after she reconnected with an old sweetheart online." She smiled, thrilled that her aunt had found happiness again since her husband had passed away many years ago.

"With all the social networks, it's easy to find

someone online," he said. "Have you tried to find Howard?"

"No." Tommy knew more about the Internet than she did; she only did her homework on the computer.

"You could," he said. "It probably wouldn't take you long if you searched networks for his graduating class from high school or from college."

"I probably could have found him online," she admitted. But again, fear had held her back. If she'd known where he was, she would have felt compelled to make a decision about contacting him and even guiltier if she'd still chosen to keep him and Tommy apart. "I could now, but I don't want to know just where he is. I want to know who he is."

"But if you found him online, you could e-mail him," Chance pointed out.

"And trust that he's telling me the truth when I ask him questions?"

He nodded with sudden understanding. "Oh. You don't want me to just find him for you. You want me to check him out."

"I can't tell him about Tommy. I can't trust him with my son…unless I know he's worthy of my trust," she explained. "Tommy's my whole world. I need to know if Keith is worthy of Tommy."

"I understand," Chance assured her.

"You do understand," she said, releasing a shuddery sigh of relief. "And you don't hate me."

"I could never hate you," he said. "And neither does Tommy. He was just upset."

"But you calmed him down. You comforted him the way you've been comforting me tonight," she said. "Thank you." But saying the words wasn't enough to express her gratitude. She rose up on tiptoe and pressed her lips to his.

"Jessie…" His voice, and his deep blue eyes, held a warning. But before she could heed it and step back, his arms slid around her back and pulled her closer. He clutched her against the hard muscles of his chest. Then he lowered his head and he kissed her back.

He really kissed her, like she'd been longing for him to do. His lips moved against hers with all the desire that she'd tried denying she felt for him. But watching him these past couple of weeks with Tommy, seeing his patience and kindness, she was afraid that she'd gone beyond just wanting him.

She lifted her arms and wound them around his shoulders and then slid her fingers into the hair at his nape. As she'd thought when she'd first seen him, his hair was just long enough for her to lose her fingers in the softness and thickness of the dark strands. Overwhelmed with pleasure, she gasped, and he deepened their kiss. His tongue slid across her bottom lip and into her mouth.

She shivered, and her pulse raced. While she'd been imagining this kiss for weeks, her daydreams hadn't come close to the reality. Unsettled, she pulled back. "This is a mistake."

With a ragged breath, he nodded. His forehead bumped against hers; their heads were still so close together, close enough for them to keep kissing. "It is a mistake," he agreed.

She winced. "Thanks…"

"I want you," Chance insisted, his hands shaking slightly as he cupped her face in his big palms. "But I have so much going on—with Matthew coming and this custody battle with Robyn."

"I'm sorry," she said, pulling away from him as remorse struck her. "I shouldn't have asked you to help me. It was selfish when you're so busy and need to focus on your son."

Chance caught her hands in his and tugged her back against his chest. "I'm the sheriff, remember? It's my job to help the citizens of Forest Glen."

"That's all I am?"

He sighed. "It's all you can be. Because, in my personal life, I need to focus only on my son. And you need to focus on yours."

"Yes," she agreed, her stomach churning as she considered what she was about to do. "I do need to focus on Tommy." Finding his dad was about to turn his life, as well as hers, upside down.

"So it wouldn't be fair for us to start something we may not be able to take any further than…"

"The bedroom?" she finished for him.

He groaned and released her hands. "Don't tempt me."

"I should go," she said. Before she threw herself at him again.

"What about Tommy?"

She glanced toward the open door. The poor kid was so exhausted he hadn't stirred at all. "I'll let him sleep and get him in the morning, if that's okay with you."

"You could stay, too."

Desire slammed through her along with shock at his suggestion. "Chance!"

"I'm not asking you to sleep with me," he assured her, although his eyes glinted with the same desire tingling inside her. "You can use the lower bunk in Matthew's room."

"I might as well share your bed."

"What?" His jaw dropped.

Heat rushed to her face with embarrassment. "I mean—I won't. But people will think that I have...if my car is parked in your driveway overnight."

"You care what people think?" he asked, a challenge in his voice.

"I moved to a small town as a pregnant teenager," she reminded him. "I had to stop myself from caring, so that I could live my life."

"So live your life."

If she could live the life she wanted, instead of sharing a bunk bed, she'd be sharing Chance's bed. With him.

THE CLINK of ceramic against wood drew Chance's attention from the computer screen as Eleanor placed a mug of steaming coffee on the corner of his desk. "You don't need to do that," he reminded her.

"You look like you could use it," the older woman said as she dropped into the chair across from him. "Did you have a late night?" Her eyes twinkled as if she already knew the answer to her question.

He had tossed and turned all night because Jessie had slept in a bed just a room away from his. Too close. Too beautiful. Too...desirable.

His chair creaked as he leaned back and sighed. "Jessie was right. This is a small town."

"But not small-minded," Eleanor assured him. "Whatever's going on between the two of you is your business. And hers."

"And apparently everyone else's."

Eleanor chuckled. "People might be curious. They might talk. But they don't judge."

He laughed now. "There's nothing to judge." Not that he hadn't been tempted. "I was just helping Jessie out with Tommy. He fell asleep at my house."

"So she stayed, too?"

"In the bunk with him." But he would have rather had her share his bed. Even now, as he thought about their kiss, about the softness of her lips, the sweetness of her mouth, his pulse raced.

"You didn't need to explain anything to me," his secretary told him.

He grinned. "Yeah, I didn't. But I'm hoping that you can spread the word. I don't want tongues wagging about me and Jessie Phillips."

Eleanor rose from the chair. "You know, it wouldn't be a bad thing if there was something for those tongues to wag about. Jessie's a wonderful mother, but a boy should have a man in his life, a father figure."

"I'm looking for his father," he said with another glance at his computer screen. Could it have really been this easy? Had he already found him? And why did finding Tommy's father, Jessie's high school sweetheart, fill him with this sick feeling, something almost as bitter and impalpable as jealousy?

"Even though you made that promise to Tommy, you really shouldn't go behind Jessie's back like this," Eleanor said with the brutal honesty that Chance appreciated. "If she doesn't want Tommy to know who his father is, you shouldn't get involved."

"She asked me—" He glanced up from the computer monitor and noticed the man leaning against the doorjamb. "Hey."

"There was no one out front, so I just showed myself back here," Trenton Sanders explained as he walked into the room.

Chance introduced his secretary to his lawyer and studied his old friend as the two of them shook hands. Either the big-city lawyer had protested too much about his hatred of small towns, or he kept visiting because he was worried about Chance. His gut tightened with dread. Oh, God, did he have bad news he hadn't wanted to deliver over the phone?

"That coffee smells great." Trenton flashed his patented charming lawyer grin at Eleanor. "I'd love a cup, too."

"You don't have to get his coffee, either," Chance told his secretary, but she left with a smile and a promise to bring their visitor back a cup. "So what are you doing here?" His stomach knotted even more. "Don't tell me that Robyn changed her mind. She's not letting Matthew come for a visit."

"No, that's not it," Trenton assured him as he settled into the chair Eleanor had vacated.

"What is it that brought you up to the *boonies* again?" he asked, reminding his friend of his earlier comments about the town Chance wanted to call home.

"I'm beginning to understand what you hate about the city," Trenton admitted. "About the buildings and concrete making you feel as if you can't breathe."

Chance grinned. "You're starting to like it here."

"I wouldn't go that far." Trenton shuddered. "I just need to get out of the office and the courtroom every once in a while."

"Yeah," Chance said with heavy sarcasm. "That worked out well for you in the past."

"Nearly got me killed in Afghanistan—would have, if not for you," Trenton said. "I owe you."

"No, you don't," Chance argued as he always did. "You would have done the same for me. So I'm still going to pay you for representing me in this custody battle."

The lawyer shrugged again. "Whatever. I'm not worried about the bill. I'm worried about winning."

"Me, too."

"So listen to your secretary," Trenton said. "Don't get involved with this woman."

"You were eavesdropping?"

Unrepentant, his friend nodded. "Good thing, too. You didn't tell me anything about her."

"There's nothing…" But Chance couldn't finish the lie.

Trenton sighed. "I take it she's the redhead I saw you with?"

He nodded.

"And she's got a kid she's been keeping away from his father?"

Chance sighed now. "Yeah…"

"If Robyn or her lawyer found that out, do you know how it would look in court—that you're involved with a woman who's doing the exact same thing as your ex?"

"We're not involved," he said again.

Trenton relaxed in his chair. "Good, because it would be crazy for you to get into a relationship with a woman just like your ex."

"Yeah, it would be crazy." Even though Jessie was nothing like Robyn, he couldn't fall for her—not when both their lives were unsettled. But he worried that it might already be too late.

Chapter Nine

"So how was he?" Belinda asked, peering over the rim of her wineglass.

"Fine," Jessie replied. "He's so sweet-natured that he got over being mad at me very quickly." And because she'd felt so bad, she hadn't punished Tommy for running away. He was spending the night at Christopher's this Friday.

"Sweet-natured?" Her cousin gave an unladylike snort of derision. "Well, a guy's temper definitely improves once you give him what he wants."

Jessie sighed. "I hope it's what he wants."

"He hasn't called you again?"

"Called me?" Jessie had only had a sip of her wine, not enough to be this confused, but she still pushed the glass toward the center of the coffee table, where a pizza box sat. "I just walked him down to the Johnsons' before you got here."

Belinda threw back her blond hair and erupted with laughter. "You're talking about Tommy!"

"Of course. Who were you talking about?"

Her cousin wiped tears from her green eyes. "I was talking about Sheriff Drayton." She lifted the wine bottle from the table and topped off Jessie's glass with the sweet red that she'd sworn would complement their sausage and peppers pizza. "And I want you to talk about him, too. Details, please. I'm living vicariously through you, you know."

Jessie laughed now. "Then you're living a pretty boring life."

"So he was a disappointment?"

Jessie took the wineglass from her cousin's hand. "I think you've had enough of that tonight." Bee had definitely had more than a sip.

"My first glass," Belinda reminded her. "C'mon, quit being stingy with the details. Everybody in Forest Glen knows you spent the night at the sheriff's."

Jessie shook her head, swinging her ponytail back and forth. "It wasn't like that and you know it. I was at your house when I called him and found out my son was with him. Tommy fell asleep over there. I stayed until he woke up. That's all that happened."

Her cousin studied her through eyes narrowed in skepticism. "Really?"

Unable to lie to her face, Jessie turned away and nodded. "Really."

"What the hell's the matter with you?" Belinda said, lightly smacking Jessie's shoulder. "The man's gorgeous and interested."

She couldn't deny that he was gorgeous. "He's not interested in me," she told herself as well as her cousin. "He has a lot going on right now. And so do I."

"You could have a lot going on with him," Belinda persisted. "I saw the way you looked at him at the town council meeting. I don't blame you. Every woman in Forest Glen, myself included, looks at him like that. But I've never seen you do that with anyone else. Ever since you had Tommy, you've lived only for him and have never been interested in anything—or anyone—for yourself."

"That's not true," Jessie said defensively. "Raising a child alone takes time and energy, that's all." It didn't need to be that way. Even though Keith hadn't wanted her to be pregnant, he might have accepted his son if he'd known about him. And he probably would now, once Chance found him and he met Tommy and realized how special the little boy was.

"You need more in your life than your child," Belinda argued. "Trust me."

Maybe her cousin was right, because once she told Keith about Tommy, she'd have to give him visitation rights—unless he was so angry that he sued her for full custody of their son—and then she would have time on her own. "I won't worry about that now," she said, talking to herself again.

"But you have an opportunity now," Belinda said. "Because he looks at you the same way you look at him."

"I don't know what you're talking about." Jessie shook her head, in denial of her cousin's claim and her own feelings. "*You* don't know what you're talking about."

"But I do recognize that look," Belinda admitted. "It's all about the attraction and fascination and the fear of falling in love."

"You don't understand," Jessie said.

"No, I don't. Because even though I got burned, I'd go for it again," she admitted.

"It?"

"Love."

Jessie shook her head. "Chance Drayton is not falling for me."

"Not yet," Belinda replied. "But I think he could—if you gave him the *chance*." She winked at the play on his name.

"He doesn't want that," Jessie insisted. "He is *not* interested in me." Not beyond that kiss they'd shared— the one that had haunted her nearly every moment since she'd spent the night at his house.

"Sure…" Belinda giggled. "He's not interested."

"That's right!"

"What about you?" the other woman persisted. "Do you want…Chance?"

The phone rang and saved Jessie from having to make any more denials. Anxious to escape her cousin's teasing, she grabbed up the cordless without checking to see who was calling. "Hello?"

"Jessie?"

Her pulse quickened, but she steadied her voice, not wanting to broadcast her reaction to the sheriff's call to her nosy cousin. "Yes?"

"It's Chance," he needlessly identified himself. "I'm sorry I haven't phoned earlier."

"I figured you would when you found out something." Her heart constricted. She hadn't doubted Chance would find Tommy's dad; she just hadn't believed he'd do it so quickly and that she would have to deal with the consequences of the choices she'd made so soon. "You found him?"

"I'm not calling about Keith."

She glanced out the window toward the Johnsons' house. "Is it Tommy?" She hadn't just walked him down the sidewalk; she'd gone inside and had watched him carry his bag up to Christopher's room. Had he run away from the Johnsons?

Maybe she should have told him that she'd asked Chance to find his father. But she hadn't wanted to build up his hopes, only to have them dashed if it wasn't possible to locate Keith. There was always the possibility something horrible had happened to him in the past eight years. As she'd told Chance, she hadn't searched for her ex-boyfriend at all—not on the online social networks or in obituaries, either. She had no idea where Keith was or what might have become of him. Or if he would want anything to do with the son he'd never known about…

"No, I'm calling about Matthew."

"Did his mother cancel the visit?" she asked, her heart hurting for Chance now. He would be so disappointed if he had to wait any longer to see his son.

Belinda rose from the couch and stepped in front of Jessie to mouth, "Is it him?"

She shook her head and mouthed back, "Not now."

Chance released a shuddery sigh. "No. He's coming as planned. Tomorrow."

"That's great," she said with relief. But Chance stayed ominously silent. "Isn't it great?"

"I hope it is."

"It will be."

"I want everything to be perfect," he said.

"Did we forget something?" she asked, mentally reviewing all they'd done. "Don't you think he'll have everything he needs?"

"I don't know," Chance said. "I don't know my son anymore. It might be uncomfortable with just the two of us. Could you and Tommy be here…when he gets dropped off?"

She caught herself from shouting out the *yes* she longed to utter. "I want to meet Matthew," she said. But most of all she wanted to see Chance's face when he saw his boy again, wanted to be there for him if he needed support or comfort. "But we can't be there when he gets dropped off."

"No? You have other plans."

"No," she admitted. "It should be just the two of you then and probably for the first few days. You need to reconnect, and Tommy and I would just be in the way."

"You wouldn't—"

"You two need some time alone to get to know each other again," she pointed out. As Chance had told her after they'd kissed, they each needed to focus on their child. She didn't want to distract him from that.

She could hear his sigh through the phone. "You're right. Of course you're right. It's just that…"

"You want everything to be perfect, and it will be," she assured him, "if it's just the two of you."

"Thanks." He sighed again. "Thanks for everything." He clicked off before she could say anything else. But she wouldn't be able to forget that he called.

And apparently neither would her cousin. Belinda stood in front of her, gaze focused on Jessie's face.

"You don't understand what that was about," she began, trying to forestall more false assumptions.

"There are no secrets in Forest Glen," Belinda reminded her. "I know that his son is coming to visit him."

"Then you know why I can't be there. After all this

time that they haven't seen each other, it should be just the two of them for a while."

"But it's not going to be just the two of them," Belinda pointed out. "His ex-wife will probably be there, too, dropping off their son."

Jessie shrugged as if it didn't matter to her that Chance would once again be seeing the woman whom he'd once loved enough to marry, with whom he'd had a child. If seeing each other again brought back their old feelings, it was none of her business. "So what if she is?"

"So maybe you should be, too," Belinda suggested. "Stake your claim, you know."

Incredulous, Jessie laughed. "I have no claim to stake."

"That's what you think."

JESSIE WAS RIGHT. He needed to do this alone, and he'd never felt more alone than he did now. He paced the length of his front porch, waiting for Robyn's lawyer to drop off his son for their weeklong visit. A week wasn't going to be enough time to make up for all they'd lost. That was why he wanted full custody—not out of spite, but because he'd vowed to devote himself to being Matthew's father. While Robyn was always at the hospital, too busy to even drive their son up for his visit, Chance didn't need to be in the sheriff's office 24/7. All he needed was his cell, and Mrs. Applegate's driver's license, to maintain law and order in quiet, crime-free Forest Glen.

The purr of a powerful engine drew Chance's attention to the street as Trenton pulled his sports car into the driveway. Now he regretted any ribbing he'd given his friend for being a high-priced lawyer. Trenton deserved every dollar and then some of his fee. Chance hadn't expected him to show up today for support. But as well as being a good friend, the big-city lawyer seemed to be curiously drawn to the country.

Chance had expected Jessie might come despite what she'd told him last night on the phone. Pushing aside his friend's warning against getting involved with her, he'd called her in a moment of weakness. He'd needed her comfort and support. But she'd refused—with good reason.

Still, he was relieved that Trenton had shown up. But the passenger's door opened before the driver's and a boy stepped out of the low-slung car. Trenton had driven him instead? Chance's breath caught. It couldn't be Matthew. He couldn't have gotten so tall—not in the little over a year that they hadn't seen each other. His legs trembling slightly, Chance descended the porch steps to the walkway. "Matthew?"

The kid's eyes widened, and his dark head bobbed in a brief nod. He stared back at Chance, as if unable to believe what he was seeing, too.

Did Chance look different to him? Had he aged so much during his last deployment that his son didn't recognize him? He wouldn't have put it past Robyn to have wiped out all trace of Chance from their lives: the pictures, and the letters and e-mails he'd sent from Afghanistan.

"Hey, kid," Chance greeted him, his voice choked with the emotion overwhelming him. "I'm your dad."

"I know." The boy spoke quietly, his voice quavering slightly.

"Of course he remembers you," Trenton assured

Chance, as if the lawyer represented the kid now. "He remembers everything about you."

Tears stung Chance's eyes. Maybe he was rushing things, but he couldn't stop himself from reaching out for his son. Instead of drawing back in resentment, as he'd feared, Matthew threw his arms around Chance's waist and clung to him.

Just as Tommy had cried in the tree house, Matthew cried now. Silently. Tears streaked down his face while his slight shoulders shook with the sobs he was too proud to release.

"I remember everything about you," Chance told him. "Everything from the minute you were born— two weeks early because you were too impatient to wait for your due date. I remember when you took your first step, around the coffee table. You fell against it and had to get five stitches above your eyebrow."

Matthew pulled back and wiped his face on his sleeve. Then he touched the faint scar above his dark brow. "You remember that?"

Chance nodded. "Everything."

"Everything that happened while you lived with us," Matthew said, "before you went away. You don't know what happened after you left."

Chance shook his head, his heart hurting from the loss they had both suffered. "I'm sorry. I didn't want to leave you, but I felt like I needed to go."

"To protect me and all those other people," Matthew said with a quick glance at Trenton.

His friend had no doubt spent the three-hour drive from Chicago telling Matthew all kinds of war stories— stories Chance would have preferred his son never had to hear. "I thought your mom's lawyer was bringing you up," he said.

Matthew shook his head. "I didn't want to ride with her. She's not very nice. So I begged Mom to let me ride with Mr. Sanders."

"That was very nice of your mother to agree." And nothing short of a miracle, given how Robyn felt about him and his friends; unlike Matthew, she hadn't understood why they'd actually wanted their guard deployed. She hadn't understood that they'd wanted to do their part in defending their country. "But I don't care how you got here," Chance admitted. "I'm just so glad you're here." He pulled his son in for another hug.

And the boy, despite being older than Tommy, who often claimed he was too old to suffer his mother's frequent displays of affection, clung to him, too.

Over his head, Chance mouthed "Thank you" to his friend.

SOMETHING JUMPED AROUND in Tommy's stomach when he and his mom climbed the steps to Chance's front porch. It wasn't butterflies; that'd be crazy. Had to be nerves…because sometimes when he got worried about something and couldn't eat, his mom told him he had a nervous stomach.

Maybe she was right about this, too—about leaving Chance and his son alone. But waiting three days before meeting Matthew had been driving Tommy crazy. Since it was spring break, he hadn't even had school to take his mind off Matthew playing alone in the tree house and sleeping alone in those bunk beds. And Tommy not even knowing what he was like…if he was as cool as his dad was.

Tommy missed Chance, too. He'd gone too long without seeing him. But maybe they shouldn't have interrupted him and his son. Maybe Chance would be mad at them. He had his real son now; he didn't need Tommy to play catch or build tree houses. He had Matthew.

And Matthew would probably be really mad, too, that it was Tommy who'd helped build the tree house, and got his dad unrusty playing catch, and slept first in the bunk beds. He probably wouldn't like Tommy at all—let alone want to be like a big brother so that they could all be like a real family.

"Can you knock, honey?" his mom asked. Her arms were wrapped around a brown grocery bag full of all the food she'd cooked. She'd made the cookies Tommy loved, the ones with the big chocolate chunks instead of puny chips. But his stomach had been too nervous for him to eat any of them, even when they'd been all gooey from the oven.

He hadn't touched the lasagna, either, and he really liked peeling off the cheese that burned up against the sides of the pan. When Mom had offered him the cookies and cheese, he'd told her he wanted to wait to eat with Chance and Matthew. But she'd warned him that the Draytons might not invite them to stay. That since Matthew was only going to be here a week, that he might want his dad all to himself.

Tommy didn't blame him. If Chance was his dad, he probably wouldn't want to share him with some strange little kid, either. But if that kid was his brother, it'd be different—he wouldn't be getting just a dad but a whole family.

"Honey?" his mom asked. She shifted the bag of food into one arm and lifted her hand and knocked. Then she focused on him again. "Everything all right? Do you feel okay? You wouldn't eat earlier, and you look kind of pale right now." She brushed her hand over his forehead, probably checking to see if he had a fever.

Tommy's throat too dry to swallow, he just nodded.

Her free arm slid around his shoulders now, and she squeezed. As he leaned against her, he felt her heart pounding really hard—like she was nervous, too. But before he could ask her about it, the door opened.

Chance's body blocked the light from inside the house and anything Tommy might have been able to see around him—like his son. His deep voice rumbled out with surprise, "Hey. I didn't think you were coming."

"We didn't want to intrude," his mom replied. "But we wanted to bring some things by and make sure you're getting enough to eat."

"Is that someone else bringing food?" another voice asked. "What is it this time?"

Chance turned to the side so the boy could look out, too. Like his mom had warned Tommy, they hadn't gotten invited inside yet. It was weird. When he and his mom had been working on the house, they'd sometimes just walked in without even knocking. Well, he had. Mom hadn't. And she'd tried to stop him before he'd thrown open the door.

So it was really funny that tonight he hadn't even been able to knock, like some baby. He wasn't a baby, though. He cleared his throat and answered the kid's question. "Mom made cookies—the really good kind— and she doesn't leave 'em in the oven so long that they get dried out and hard."

"Cool," the kid answered, like he meant it. He looked

like a short version of Chance with the same blue eyes and black hair instead of Tommy's weird orangish-red.

"I also brought lasagna," his mom said with a smile. "And a salad."

At the mention of vegetables, Tommy crossed his eyes and squeezed his lips sideways. Matthew laughed at his fish face.

Chance chuckled and said, "You didn't have to bring us dinner."

"No," Mom agreed.

"But we really appreciate it," Chance said, and he took the bag from her hands. "Thank you." He glanced down at his son, and his eyes smiled, like he was so happy he was busting. And proud. That must be how dads looked at their sons.

Tommy sighed.

"Matthew." Chance said the kid's name like he looked at him, with love and pride and happiness. "These are my very good friends—Jessie Phillips and her son, Tommy."

Tommy glanced up at the sheriff. Had Chance just said his name like he had Matthew's? Like he was proud of him? Like he was happy he was there? Like he might love him?

No. Tommy must have imagined it. It wasn't like he was Chance's son or anything. He had his own dad out there. Somewhere.

"It was Tommy's idea to build the tree house for you," Chance was explaining to Matthew. "He designed it and helped me build it."

"Cool," Matthew said again—like he meant it. "I've never seen a real tree house before. I can't believe I got one. Do you have one?"

Tommy shook his head. "No. We don't have any trees big enough."

"So we'll share mine," Matthew offered, "since you worked so hard on it."

Tommy fought the frogs out of his voice. "That'd be great."

"Want to go up now?" Matthew asked him. He didn't wait for Tommy's answer before he turned to his dad. "Can we hang out in the tree house for a little while?"

Chance looked at Tommy's mom. "Can the two of you stay for a while?"

"Sure," she said and stepped inside the house and reached for the bag again. "I can warm up the lasagna and put the salad into bowls."

"Then you'll have to eat with us," Chance said.

Tommy blew out a breath he hadn't known he was holding. They hadn't just got invited inside; they'd gotten asked to stay for dinner and to play. This was what he'd been dreaming about ever since Chance had told Tommy his son was coming to visit.

"What about your dad?" Matthew asked Tommy as they headed through the house to the backyard.

"What do you mean?" Tommy asked.

"Is he gonna come over and eat with us, too?"

Tommy shook his head. "Nah, I don't have a dad."

"You don't?"

"Well, I never met him." He waited for Matthew to offer to share Chance like he'd offered to share the tree house. But the kid didn't say anything about that; he just opened the back door and headed out into the yard.

Tommy didn't blame him. Sharing a tree house was one thing. But sharing his dad…

Chapter Ten

"I thought you weren't coming," Chance said over his shoulder as Jessie followed him down the hall to the kitchen. "Matthew's been here for three days already, and you didn't even call."

Was that hurt she glimpsed in the depths of his dark blue eyes? Or was she just imagining it?

"We always intended to come over and meet your son. I just thought you needed a few days to get to know each other again. And your first meeting with Matthew definitely needed to be just the two of you." She bit her lip to hold in the question she was dying to ask. *But had it been just the two of them? Or had his ex-wife been here, too?*

"It was," he replied, as if he'd instinctively known what she was dying to ask. "Well, except for my lawyer. He drove Matthew up from Chicago."

"His mother wasn't able to come?"

"She couldn't get away from the hospital."

"Hospital? Is she all right?" Jessie felt guilty that she'd been a little bit—okay, more than a little bit— jealous of the woman.

"She's fine—she's a doctor," he said with nearly the same pride with which he'd introduced his son.

"Oh, that's impressive." Especially to Jessie, who'd been struggling to take one night class per semester. But, with Belinda babysitting Tommy while she was at class or needed time to study, Jessie had kept at it the past seven years and would soon have her nursing degree.

"Let's hope the judge doesn't think so, too," he murmured as he placed the bag on the butcher-block counter that complemented the white cabinets and the pale yellow walls of the country kitchen.

"You're impressive," she assured him. "You're a Marine and a lawman." If Keith had become even half of the man Chance had, she'd probably lose if he took her to court for Tommy. But she hadn't done a bad job as a single parent. Until her son had gotten fixated on finding his father, he'd been a happy, well-adjusted boy.

"So you think I can win this custody battle?" Chance asked as he stared out the window, watching the boys climb the rope ladder into the tree house.

"I think you can," she admitted, then wondered aloud, "But do you really want to?"

His dark brows furrowed. "What are you saying? Do you think that I really don't want my son? I just asked you to be here because I was worried that it would be awkward. But it wasn't. It was like we'd hardly been apart—well, except for how much he's grown."

"I know you want him to live with you," she said. "But do you really want to take him away from his mother?"

"This isn't about you, Jessie."

She sucked in a breath in reaction to the sting of his remark. "No, it's not," she agreed. Her hand shaking, she reached for the handle of the back door. "So Tommy and I should go…"

Chance covered her hand with his, and his chest pressed against her back. His breath stirred her hair as he said, "I'm sorry."

She resisted the urge to lean back against him, to let his strength and warmth envelope her. No matter how attracted she was to him, they had no business being together.

"I didn't mean that the way it sounded," he continued. "I just meant that you're not Robyn and I'm not Keith. And you can't compare our situations."

"What about you?" she asked. "You've admitted that you did exactly that."

"I know," he said with a heavy sigh. "And I was wrong."

"Yes. You were."

"So don't do the same to me," he said. "Don't judge me."

She allowed the tension to leave her body and melted against his chest. "Okay."

"So you'll stay."

"Do you want us to stay?"

He tightened his arms around her and lowered his head until his lips brushed her ear. "Yes…"

CHANCE DIDN'T JUST WANT Jessie to stay. He wanted her. Period. And maybe because of that he should have let her leave. But as the evening wore on, he was happy that she and Tommy had stayed. He'd thought of everything for his son but a friend.

And even though Tommy was younger than Matthew, the boys bonded. But as he'd noticed the first time he'd met Tommy Phillips, the kid had a maturity and determination far beyond his years. He also had that funny, charming personality that made people want to be his friend. So Chance wasn't surprised that Matthew genuinely liked Tommy.

He was surprised by how much Matthew seemed to like Jessie. He raved over her lasagna and even the salad, having two helpings of each. And when he bit into a cookie, he sighed with ecstasy, as excited as if he'd never had a cookie before in his life. Chance had to tease him about his reaction, even as he sighed in enjoyment himself when he bit into one.

Color flooded Matthew's face. "I don't mean to act like a pig, but Mom doesn't let me eat like this."

"I'm sorry," Jessie said, her eyes widening with regret. "Aren't you supposed to have sugar? Does your mom think it's bad for your health?"

Matthew laughed. "No, bad for her apartment. She and Mrs. Ruiz, the housekeeper, think sweets make me too hyper and that I might break something in the house."

"That's why Mom makes me play outside," Tommy said. In an apparent imitation of his mother, he pitched his voice high and squeaky and added, "No balls in the house. No skateboarding in the living room."

"You skateboard?" Matthew asked.

Tommy nodded and then laughed. "Just not very good."

"I can show you," Matthew offered. "We have a skateboarding park around the corner from our apartment. I don't get to it that much because Mrs. Ruiz won't let me walk down there by myself. She and Mom think I'll get shot or something. But I know some tricks."

"So you like your bedroom?" Jessie asked, changing the subject away from the drive-bys, probably because she'd noticed Chance's tension. Matthew not being able to play safely outside was just one of the reasons he wanted to move his son to Forest Glen.

"I love my room!" Matthew answered enthusiastically.

"Jessie painted it for you," Chance said. "She worked really hard on it."

Matthew glanced from him to Jessie and back, as if wondering if they were more than friends. The kid wasn't the only one asking himself that. Chance was, too.

"Thank you," Matthew told her.

"You're welcome," Jessie warmly replied. "But no one worked as hard as your father did. He wanted everything to be perfect for you."

The tree house, the room and bunk beds—Chance had done all that for Matthew. But sitting around the table and talking with the people he cared about made everything perfect for Chance. The house he'd inherited finally felt like his home.

The apartment he'd shared with Robyn hadn't been home for him and apparently her new place wasn't home for Matthew. This house should be the boy's home, and these people his family. Chance had to win the custody case. Emotion overwhelmed him, so much so that he welcomed the ringing doorbell.

Matthew groaned and rubbed his stomach. "That's probably someone else bringing food."

"Probably," Jessie agreed as she stood up and began to clear the table.

"It's nice of them," Matthew said, as he rose from his chair and brought his dish to the sink where Jessie stood. "But it won't be as good as yours."

On his way to the door, Chance glanced back and noticed Jessie slide her arm around his son's shoulders and squeeze. Matthew, obviously no fool, leaned against her. For a minute, Chance was actually jealous of his son—that his relationship with Jessie could be so uncomplicated. With a sigh of self-disgust, Chance pulled open the front door. His jaw dropped open in shock as he recognized his gray-haired visitor. "Hello, Mrs. Wilson."

Even though he'd been living in Forest Glen awhile, he hadn't realized how much the townspeople would support him during his son's visit. He hadn't expected any of the casseroles and pies that so many of his neighbors had dropped off. But this woman was the last person he'd figured would come bearing baked goods. Sure enough, though, she held a basket in her arms.

"I brought you something," she said in her usual brusque, unfriendly manner. "Well, I brought it for you and your boy." She glanced toward the small SUV parked behind his recently repaired police car. "And I guess Jessie Phillips' boy, too."

"That wasn't necessary, Mrs. Wilson," he assured her. "You didn't need to bring us anything."

"Sure I did," she insisted. "Every kid needs a pet. And you know I have too many to take care of myself. Dang fool things getting caught up in tractors and car engines and such."

Chance suppressed a groan because he'd probably need to save his breath if he was right about what she had in the basket hooked over her arm. "Really, it isn't necessary," he said again.

"Well, if you decide not to keep it, you can drop it off at the animal shelter," she said, staring at the basket in confusion. "I don't know why someone dropped this thing off at my house. It's not like I don't have more than enough furry critters."

"That's probably why animals are dropped at your house," he pointed out. "People know how much you love them—too much to part with any of them." He hoped. He'd already made more than his share of trips to the doctor's office.

"I have no problem parting with this kind of critter," she insisted. "And your boy will love it."

"He might have the same allergies I have," Chance warned her. If he was any kind of father, he'd know if his son had allergies and to what. When Jessie had asked Matthew about sugar, he'd had no clue if his son followed a restricted diet. Robyn wouldn't even talk to him.

"I think this is one of those hypoallergenic, nonshedding kind," Mrs. Wilson assured him as she pulled the furry critter from her basket. The ball of curly yellow fur whined and yipped and licked her fingers.

Chance studied her face, wondering how she knew so much about a stray—a dog, no less—that had been dropped on her property. Had she bought the puppy from a pet store just for his son?

"A puppy!" the boys yelled as they headed down the hall from the kitchen. Both of them ran, skidding in their socks, to the foyer. Barking with excitement, the tiny dog squirmed free of the old woman's grasp and jumped onto the kids who knelt on the hardwood floor to play with him.

"I think they like it," Mrs. Wilson said with a smile of satisfaction and pleasure. She dropped the basket onto the porch. "There's food and a leash and some other stuff in there." The dog was definitely no stray; she had bought it for him.

"Can we keep it?" Matthew asked, his eyes so round with hopefulness that Chance couldn't say no.

He nodded his acceptance. He couldn't disappoint his son or the woman who'd gone to so much trouble to buy him the perfect pet.

"Thank you, ma'am," Matthew sincerely told Mrs. Wilson, while Tommy, apparently too overwhelmed for words, threw his arms around her and hugged tight.

The old lady stumbled back a step with shock. Then her swollen fingers patted the boy's red head. "You're welcome, honey."

Chance stumbled as his son threw his arms around his waist. "Thanks, Dad. Everything is perfect."

Over his son's head, he met Jessie's gaze as she joined all of them in the foyer. She understood and shared the moment of celebration with him, but he also noticed the concern in her gaze. She was as worried as he was that this might be the only visit he had with his son.

"So my cookies have been replaced," Jessie said as she gazed over Chance's makeshift gate into the utility room, where he'd imprisoned the whining labradoodle puppy.

"They named him Cookie," Chance reminded her, leaning over her shoulder to stare down at the puppy.

She tilted her head to gaze back at him, her breath stalling as she found his face very close—nearly close enough to kiss. "Are you sure you've done the right thing?"

"They'll be fine out there in the tree house," he assured her. "It's warm tonight, and I made sure the trapdoor was closed. No one's going to fall out of the tree."

"I wasn't talking about the boys," she said. But she wasn't totally convinced that she should have agreed to let them spend the night ten feet in the air. "I meant with the puppy."

His sigh stirred her hair and raised goose bumps along her skin. "After that allergic reaction, I'm not crazy about things with fur. But you saw how excited the boys got."

"How hard will it be for Matthew to leave Cookie here when he has to go home?" she asked.

Chance stepped away from her. "I hope it's me he's going to miss more than the dog."

"I'm sure he will miss you," Jessie said. "But Robyn might think that getting him a dog wasn't playing fair."

Would Keith play games with her when he found out about Tommy? Would he compete with her to be the better, more fun parent? Not that Chance had gone out and purchased the puppy; she suspected Mrs. Wilson had done that. No one gave away a specialty-bred dog unless there was a sweet, generous soul hidden beneath her gruff exterior. But Chance had built the tree house and bought all the video games and sporting equipment his son and hers had been playing with all night.

"Not at all," Chance said. "I didn't plan on giving him that puppy."

"I know," she said. "I know. I'm sorry…"

He pushed a hand through his hair, disheveling the dark strands. "This is so hard," he said, as he turned away from her. "Too hard. Seeing my son again, being with him…" His voice cracked with emotion. "And knowing that he's only here for a few more days…and that he might not be able to come back ever again."

Jessie pressed herself against his stiff back and wrapped her arms around him. "You'll see him again. You'll have a relationship with your son."

He pulled her arms away then turned around and dragged her tight against him. "That's not the only relationship I want right now."

She tipped up her face but held her mouth back from touching his. "I thought you considered this—that you considered us—a mistake."

"I wanted to focus on Matthew."

"I know—that's why I tried to stay away," she reminded him. "I didn't want to intrude."

"But you didn't have to be here to intrude. I kept thinking about you, missing you, wanting you…" He kissed her now with all the desire they'd been fighting for each other.

But just kissing wasn't going to be enough this time. For either of them. Chance swung her up in his arms while Jessie clung to him. She pulled her mouth from his to murmur, "What about the boys?"

"We'll hear them come in," he promised.

"How?"

He glanced back toward the dog. "My new alarm system courtesy of Mrs. Wilson."

She smiled even as her heart pounded frantically in anticipation as he carried her through the foyer. He started up the staircase, and with each step he climbed, that anticipation intensified and a pressure built inside her. Then he carried her through the open door of the room she'd only glanced inside when she'd been painting Matthew's.

She'd wanted to paint this room, too, to add color to the plain white walls and black sheets. But she'd refrained from offering, figuring she had no business in Chance Drayton's bedroom.

And she probably still had no business being here. He dropped his arm from beneath her legs, and she slid down the hard length of his body. He groaned and pulled her close again—so close that nothing but their clothes separated their bodies.

And then not even clothes, as they frantically lowered zippers and undid buttons. Chance took his time with her, kissing every inch of skin he exposed, until Jessie trembled with desire for him. She couldn't remember ever wanting any man as desperately as she wanted Chance.

"Please," she murmured when his lips skimmed from her neck, over her collarbone to the curve of her breast. "Chance…"

Then his mouth closed around her nipple and he gently tugged at the sensitive point. She tunneled her fingers into his soft hair, holding him against her. But she had to touch more than his hair. So she skimmed her hands down the broad expanse of his back and over his lean hips.

He lifted his head from her breast and carried her to the bed, laying her on it. But he didn't stop kissing her, his lips clinging to hers, tongue sliding over tongue and breath mingling with moans. His hands slid over her, following every curve and dip, until his fingers moved through her curls and into the very heat and essence of her desire.

She arched her hips, wanting more. Needing more. But he pulled back. A drawer opened, foil rustled, and he moved over her. His mouth covered her lips again, then skimmed across her cheek to her ear.

"Are you sure?" he asked.

She nodded and raked her nails down his back, pulling him closer.

"But I'm not sure I can offer you more than tonight," he warned her. "I don't know what the future holds for either of us."

"I know," she said. If he'd made promises or declarations of love like Keith had, she wouldn't have trusted him enough to give herself to him. "And I appreciate your honesty." Except that it forced her to be honest with herself, to admit that she was falling for him despite that uncertain future.

"I appreciate you," he said, "everything about you. Your beauty. Your generosity. Your fierce protectiveness."

Of Tommy. If she was protecting herself, she would have left after the boys had gone up to the tree house. She shouldn't have stayed alone with him, should never have allowed him to carry her to his bed.

But she wanted him too much to deny either of them. "I need you," she said. "I want you." She lifted her legs and wrapped them around his waist.

He groaned, as if his control was slipping, but carefully joined their bodies. Jessie didn't want gentleness. She wanted passion. She kissed him, her tongue sliding into his mouth as he thrust inside her body.

Lifting her hips, she met his every thrust—fighting to release the pressure building inside her. His mouth left her lips, and he contorted his body until he could reach her breasts. As he tugged at a nipple, the pressure broke. With a keening moan, she came.

Then he shuddered and groaned and collapsed on top of her. But that gentleness returned and he rolled his weight off her and clutched her to his side. His fingers trembled slightly as he stroked her shoulder. "That was…phenomenal."

And stupid. But she had no regrets…except that they couldn't spend the night making love. The boys were bound to get cold or have to use the bathroom, and they'd be back inside.

"I can't stay in your bed," she said.

He uttered a heavy sigh of regret. "I know. We don't want to confuse the boys."

It wasn't just the boys she was worried about, though. She had confused herself with all this desire, with all these feelings. But she couldn't keep doing what she wanted. She had to focus on what her son needed.

"The boys need to come first," she reminded them both. "I have to give Tommy what he wants."

Chance nodded, his chin bumping lightly against her forehead.

"I have to give him his father. I need you to find him."

His fingers stopped tracing the random pattern on her bare skin and stilled. "I have."

Chapter Eleven

With every mile he drew closer to the city, another knot formed in Chance's stomach, so that when he finally found a parking spot on the busy street outside Robyn's building, he felt cramped with dread. And with every mile Matthew had become more withdrawn, so that now he sat, sullen and silent, in the passenger seat.

"Are you okay?" Chance asked. His son didn't move at all even though he'd shut off the car.

The kid's head jerked in response, but whether it was a nod or a shake, Chance could not tell.

"Your finger all right?" he asked, gesturing toward the Band-Aid on Matthew's pinkie. Tommy Phillips had an identical injury, so Chance was pretty certain the wounds were self-inflicted and hopefully not very deep. Jessie had inspected the cuts, and she'd applied the ointment and Band-Aids. She'd met Chance's gaze and shared his concern over the bond their boys had formed.

Matthew's head bobbed forward in a definite nod this time. A lock of dark hair fell into his eyes.

"I'll get your bag," Chance offered, reaching for the door handle.

But Matthew's fingers clutched his arm, holding him back. "Will you go upstairs with me?"

"Of course," Chance readily agreed despite increasing dread over the thought of an ugly confrontation with Robyn.

"I don't want to go up," Matthew admitted, his breath hitching with tears he kept proudly blinking away.

"You have school tomorrow," Chance reminded him.

"I don't wanna go."

"Nobody wants to go back to school after spring break," he agreed. "But you have friends here. You'll have fun."

"Not as much fun as I had with you and Cookie. And Tommy and Jessie." Matthew gave a loud sniffle.

While his son's words brought Chance pleasure, they also made him feel guilty. He'd wanted Matthew's visit to be so perfect that he hadn't really considered how hard it might be for the boy to return to his regular life.

"It probably seemed like more fun because it was different than what you're used to," Chance said. "But you'll get back into your routine with school and friends."

"Mom says you're trying to take all that away from me," Matthew said, "that you're going to screw up our lives just like you did when you deployed."

Maybe Jessie was right about his battle for full custody—that he was acting out of spite rather than in the best interests of his son. "I'm sorr—"

"But Mom's wrong," Matthew said. "I like it in Forest Glen. A lot. I like my room and the yard and the tree house." His eyes sparkled. "And my puppy."

Jessie had definitely been right about that. The boy

hadn't been able to fight his tears when he'd had to say goodbye to his dog. But no pets were allowed in Robyn's apartment building, except cats.

"But that's not all I really like," Matthew continued with a glance down at the Band-Aid on his little finger. "I really like—"

Knocking sounded against the window behind Chance's head, and he whirled around. It was probably Robyn, tapping the dial of her watch to remind Chance he was a few minutes late. But, like Mrs. Applegate, he'd struggled to keep the car at the speed limit. He'd wanted to drive as slowly as he could, to savor every minute left with his son.

Some of his tension eased as he noted it wasn't Robyn but Trenton. As Chance had imagined, he was tapping the face of his expensive watch.

"You're late," the lawyer warned as Chance opened the door. "Matthew needed to be upstairs half an hour ago."

Matthew tightened his grip on Chance's arm. "You're still coming up?"

"Yes." He stepped onto the busy street next to his friend.

"I can grab his bag and walk him up," Trenton offered.

Chance reached into the backseat for his son's duffel, but he held tight to the handles despite his friend reaching for it. "No. I'm not saying goodbye to my son on the street."

Trenton leaned closer. "I was supposed to drive him back. Not you. This isn't going to go well for either of us if Robyn knows it was you."

"I don't want Matthew to lie to his mother," Chance explained. "Especially not for me."

"I'm not asking him to lie," Trenton insisted. "It's just that whole don't ask, don't tell thing."

"We both know Robyn," Chance reminded him. "She's going to ask."

Trenton laughed. "I don't think you ever really knew Robyn. That's the problem."

Chance couldn't argue with the lawyer. For one, his friend was too good at arguing. For another, he was also right. Chance never would have figured the sweet girl he'd fallen in love with in college would have become the angry, bitter woman his ex-wife was now. Obviously he had never really known her.

"Mom's probably not even here," Matthew said as they headed into the building. "She's probably at the hospital, like she always is."

"Do you have a key?" Chance asked. He hadn't seen one in his son's bag. Matthew had a cell phone and charger, though.

"Nah, Mrs. Ruiz will let me in," Matthew assured them. But after they left the elevator car and walked down the hall toward Robyn's apartment, it wasn't the housekeeper who opened the door at their knock. It was Robyn herself. With her dark hair in a close-cropped style that offset her wide eyes and delicate features, she looked younger than her thirty-three years—more like the college girl he remembered. But her jaw was clenched, her dark eyes brimming with anger and impatience as she met his gaze, and she was again the ex-wife who'd punished him for signing up for another deployment.

Then she looked at Matthew, and her eyes warmed

and glistened. She closed her arms around their son and clung tight to him. "I've missed you so much!"

Matthew hugged her back for a moment before jerking away. "You probably didn't even notice me gone," he accused her, reminding Chance of the claim Tommy Phillips had made when they had first met.

But Tommy had been wrong. And from the flash of hurt in Robyn's dark eyes, he suspected that Matthew was, too.

"You're never around," the boy said, adding insult to injury.

"Matthew, I'm going to pretend that you didn't say that," his mother replied. "You've had a long drive home, so you're probably tired—you look as if you didn't get enough rest this past week. Why don't you go to your room and lie down for a while before dinner?"

"I want to say goodbye to my dad."

Chance flinched.

"Well, I don't want to say goodbye," Matthew said, noticing his father's reaction. "But you're making me. And I don't want to. I have to."

"You have to go to your room now," Robyn said, color flooding her pale complexion. "And I'll send your father back to say goodbye before he leaves."

Matthew glared at his mother and turned to Chance for confirmation. He nodded.

"Great, you've done it already," she sniped after their son's door slammed. "You've undermined me."

"So Matthew told you about the dog?"

"Dog? You got him a dog, too?" Her voice rose in anger to the same shrill pitch Tommy had used to imitate his mom. "The tree house wasn't enough?"

"A week with my son wasn't enough, not after all the time you've kept us apart."

"C'mon, folks," Trenton said, finally breaking his uncharacteristic silence. "Making accusations isn't going to help either of you, and it's only going to upset your son. Let the lawyers handle this."

"Maybe that's the problem," Robyn said, her eyes narrowed in a waspish glare as she turned on Trenton with resentment and animosity. "Maybe we need to get the lawyers out of it and talk to each other."

"Yes," Chance agreed, but reminded her, "You're the one who's refused to take any of my calls."

Robyn sighed. "Are we going to keep playing the blame game?"

"I'm not playing games," he vowed to her, just as he had Jessie.

"No, you found other people to play the games." She snorted. "When I called him, he talked nonstop about Tommy and Jessie. Your plan worked. He had a lot of fun with those boys."

"Jessie's not a—"

"Let her talk," Trenton interrupted. "Jessie's not important."

But Chance was afraid that she was, that she was so important to him he didn't know if he would be able to give her up and move back to Chicago if he didn't win the custody battle.

"No, Jessie and Tommy aren't important," Robyn said, "because Matthew has friends here, a lot of them in the neighborhood and more at school. You can't take him away from his life."

"He can make a life with me in Forest Glen," Chance said. And the life he imagined was Matthew and he and

Tommy and Jessie sitting around the dinner table as they had that perfect night and each of the four following nights. "It's a great place for a boy to grow up."

She shook her head. "My son is not moving."

Chance's lawyer spoke for him. "That doesn't sound like a compromise."

"It's not," Chance said. And Trenton was wrong. He knew his ex-wife; he knew she didn't compromise. She was only happy if everyone did what she wanted them to do.

"The compromise is that I might agree to sharing custody," Robyn said, "if you swear you're not going back into the reserves and if you move back here."

Chance didn't respond to her offer; he was too stunned she'd made it. Instead he walked down the hall to his son's room. He knew it was Matthew's because the door was open again. The room was smaller than the one Jessie had decorated for him in the farmhouse, and it was cramped with furniture and clothes. The only thing visible out the window was the brick wall of another building and the metal of a fire escape. This was the life Chance had known: concrete and brick and the incessant noise of traffic and sirens. He'd wanted more for his son, and he could give that to him in Forest Glen.

But if he didn't win the custody battle, he wouldn't be able to give him anything. Could he risk it? Sharing custody with Robyn in Chicago would be better than not being able to see his son at all. But could he do it? Could he give up everything—and *everyone*—in Forest Glen?

He closed his arms around his boy, who clung to him. "I'll see you again," he promised. And he had never broken a promise to his son; he'd come home from

Afghanistan in one piece. "Your mother and I will work this out. You and I will spend more time together."

"I wanna spend all my time with you," Matthew said.

That had been Chance's plan, but he wasn't certain now if that was best for his son.

"It's best for the boy to share custody," Trenton said a short while later as they stepped inside the elevator car. "I can tell the mediator that we've come to an agreement, and a judge will approve joint custody with no problem."

"You're saying that I can't win full custody?"

"I'm saying that you need to move home."

But Chicago wasn't home anymore. Forest Glen—and Tommy and Jessie—was home. But he had once put other things and other people before his son when he'd signed up for the reserves and then that second deployment. He couldn't do it again. He had to put Matthew first. The boy's happiness was more important than Chance's.

JESSIE SWALLOWED a sigh as she watched her son push his food around his plate without bringing the fork to his mouth once. She couldn't blame him. The only thing she'd swallowed since they'd sat down to dinner was her wistful sigh.

"You feeling okay?" she asked.

Tommy nodded. "When will Chance be back?"

She wasn't the only one getting too attached to the ex-Marine. But even though she and Chance had made love, they couldn't plan a future together. Their lives were too complicated.

"He might be gone a couple of days," she warned her

son. Spending all that time with Chance and his son had been a mistake for both her and Tommy.

"Chicago is that far away?" he asked, his eyes wide with concern. It wasn't just Chance he missed; he and Matthew had formed an obvious bond.

"No, it's only a few hours."

"Is he going to stay there—in the city—with Matt?" Tommy asked.

Eventually. Jessie believed Chance would have to move back to Chicago if he wanted a relationship with his son. She couldn't imagine a judge removing the boy from the parent who'd been taking care of him—and judging by his sweet manners, good care—for the past year. While she commiserated with Chance's situation, she hoped a judge would also consider how well she'd raised Tommy alone if Keith sued her for custody.

"No, he's not staying in Chicago." Yet. "He's coming back to Michigan, but on his way home, he's stopping in Battle Creek for a day or two."

He'd promised to check out Keith more thoroughly than he already had online. Keith had no criminal record and worked in the accounting department of a pharmaceutical company just over an hour away from Forest Glen. He'd lived so close and yet their paths had never crossed since that day he'd kissed her goodbye when he'd left for college.

"Why can't Chance come right home?" Tommy asked. "What's in Battle Creek?"

She swallowed hard again, choking on the fear that overwhelmed her. She hadn't told him she'd asked Chance to look for Keith because she'd worried that the man might still not be ready for parenthood. But

Tommy deserved the truth, no matter what it was. "Your father."

"Who?" Tommy asked again, his pale blue eyes wide with shock.

"Your dad lives in Battle Creek."

"That's not that far away, right?" Tommy asked. "Isn't that where we saw the giraffe?"

"At the Binder Park Zoo, yes," Jessie said, surprised Tommy remembered the trip they'd made a few years ago and even more surprised that they had been so close to his father without realizing it.

"So why does Chance have to stay there so long?" Tommy asked. "We didn't have to spend the night when we drove down to the zoo."

The kid had an incredible memory. "Chance is going to talk to your dad. Before I tell him about you, we need to make sure that he'd be a good dad."

Tommy nodded. "Chance wants to make sure he's a good guy, not a crook."

She laughed at his perceptiveness. "Yes."

"I don't care."

"Well, I do, honey. I don't want him spending time with you if he's changed from the nice young man I remember."

"If he was nice, how come you didn't marry him?" he asked.

"Because he didn't love me," she admitted, knowing that back then she probably would have said yes had he proposed. But then she would have wound up like her cousin, divorced once she'd discovered what love really was. "That's why I didn't tell him about you," she explained. "I didn't want him to be with me just because of you."

Tommy nodded. Maybe he wasn't too young to understand.

"I'm sorry," she said. "I still should have told him about you. And I'm going to do that soon, once Chance comes back."

Tommy shook his head. "But I don't want *him* anymore." He jumped up and pushed back his chair with such force that it toppled over. Barking erupted as he startled the labradoodle puppy awake from its bed in the corner of the kitchen. "I don't want my dad! I want Chance to be my dad and Matt to be my brother." Tears streaked down his face. "I want Chance..."

He ran from the room, the curly-haired puppy on his heels.

Instead of chasing after them, Jessie pushed her plate toward the center of the table and laid her head on her arms. She felt like crying, too, because he wasn't the only one who wanted Chance.

"HEY," TOMMY SAID when Matthew answered the phone. "Are you home yet?"

"No."

"You're still driving?" Matthew and Chance had left early that morning because Tommy had had to get up really early for him and his mom to say goodbye. He'd cried so hard watching his new friend drive off with Chance, but that was probably because he'd been so tired.

"No, this crappy apartment isn't home," Matt replied, sounding as if he had a runny nose. "I want to come back to Forest Glen."

"Yeah, it would be so cool if you could move here," Tommy said.

"Are you taking care of Cookie?" Matt asked.

He glanced down on the floor where the little yellow dog chewed on one of his shoes. His mom wouldn't like that the new tennis shoe was all torn and slobbery. But Tommy didn't care. He wasn't too happy with his mom right now. Or with anything else.

"Yeah…but just till your dad gets back here," Tommy said. "Cookie's your dog."

"*Our* dog," Matthew corrected him. "My dad's not home yet? He left a while ago—after him and my mom got done fighting."

"They were fighting?" Tommy couldn't imagine Chance getting mad at anyone, but then Matt's mom had been keeping him away from Chance. That had probably made him mad. Would Tommy's dad be mad that his mom had kept him away from Tommy?

"Yeah." Matt sighed. "I guess it's cool that they're fighting over me, you know. That they both want me." But he didn't sound like he really thought it was cool, especially since he sniffed again. "I just think it's really lame that I can't pick."

"Who would you pick?" Tommy wondered.

"I love my mom," Matt said. "She's not around a whole lot, but she has a really important job. So I get that she's busy. But I can always call her. She never goes out of the country. If I needed her, she'd be there for me."

"So would your dad," Tommy defended Chance. "He's the sheriff. He's there for everybody."

"Mom says that's the problem," his friend explained. "He's there for everybody else but us."

Tommy didn't like Matt's mom very much. "Do you believe her?"

Matt sighed again. "I don't know who to believe,"

he admitted. "Dad promised me that he'd be part of my life now, that we'd spend time together, that I'll always come first with him."

"You can believe him," Tommy said. "He kept his promise to me."

"What promise?" Matt asked.

"The first time we met I asked him to find my real dad, and he has."

"You don't sound too happy about it."

Tommy glanced down at the Band-Aid on his hand. The wound still throbbed a bit. Becoming blood brothers had been his idea, but like finding his dad, it hadn't been a very good one. He'd cut a little deep, and the cuts hadn't stopped bleeding until his mom had bandaged them. "I don't care about my real dad anymore," he said.

"Are you scared he might be a jerk?"

He should have thought about that before he'd asked Chance to find him. "I don't know…"

"He probably has a wife and kids," Matthew warned him. "You might have little brothers and sisters."

Little kids like his cousins, who got in his stuff and lost the pieces to his puzzles and messed up the scores on his video games? No thanks.

"I'd rather have a big brother," he said. "I'd rather have you."

"We are brothers," Matt reminded him. "Mom checked out my cut. She said if it was any deeper I might have needed stitches. Isn't that cool?"

Tommy didn't think so. The cut had hurt like heck but it wasn't nearly as bad as having to say goodbye to Matt that morning. He did not want to have to do that again.

"You know what would be cool?" Tommy said. "If your dad married my mom, we could all live together in your dad's big house. We'd be a real family."

"Yeah, that would be cool," Matt agreed with a sigh. "But I wouldn't count on it happening. My mom doesn't want me to move to Forest Glen. And you don't know what's going to happen with your dad."

Finding his dad had definitely not been one of his better ideas.

Chapter Twelve

Chance drew in a deep breath and lifted his fist to knock. After a moment, the riveted steel door with the peephole in the middle opened to a man's handsome face. "Keith Howard?" he asked.

The brown-haired guy nodded. "Who are you? A process server?" He laughed at what he must have meant as a joke.

But Chance didn't join in the laughter. "Are you anticipating a lawsuit?"

Howard laughed again, but with more ironic humor than real amusement. "So you're the guy."

"Which guy?"

"The one who's been asking around about me at my office and here at the condo complex." He studied Chance's face intently. "So you know everything about me now, probably down to my shoe size, but I don't know anything about you. Care to identify yourself?"

Chance reached for the badge he hadn't had to show anyone since Mrs. Applegate smashed into his car. Since that crash, things had been quiet in Forest Glen—as he'd been warned they always were. But bringing Tommy's dad to the town would end that calm as the gossip began.

And how excited would Tommy be that Chance had kept his promise?

Certainly more excited than Chance was. Everyone he'd talked to the day before had had nothing but complimentary things to say about Keith Howard. That should have made Chance happy, given him relief, but it just filled him with regret for having found the guy.

"So are you going to show me your identification?" Howard asked.

Chance nodded and flipped his wallet open to his badge. The guy leaned closer to read it.

"Forest Glen? That's about an hour or so northwest of here, right?"

Chance nodded again.

"So what's the sheriff of Forest Glen doing asking around about me?" Keith Howard's smooth brow furrowed. He was just twenty-six, making Chance feel old and cynical. "I've never even been there. I've only noticed it as a dot on a map."

"You need to go there."

A door opened behind Chance, and he glanced over his shoulder at the neighbor peering through the crack. The condo complex was located in a converted cereal warehouse, with exposed brick and high ceilings. With a gym and a bar and restaurant, it was more a complex for singles than couples or families.

"You need to step inside," Keith said, gesturing for Chance to enter. Then he closed the door behind him. If nosy neighbors concerned him, the guy was going to hate Forest Glen.

A couple of bikes crowded the foyer of the accountant's condo. That was something Tommy and his dad had in common, that and their pale blue eyes. Keith wouldn't need a DNA test to prove that he was the boy's father.

All Chance had needed was Jessie's word. Should he have trusted her though? He'd trusted Robyn once, too, and had lost his son because of it.

"So why do I need to go to Forest Glen?" Keith asked, leading the way past the bikes and a galley kitchen into the loft-like living room. "Am I wanted for questioning or something?"

"Or something," Chance replied. He wasn't supposed to talk to Howard. He was only supposed to check him out for Jessie. And he had when he'd interviewed neighbors and coworkers. But to determine what kind of man Keith Howard truly was, Chance needed to speak with him personally. Man to man.

"I wasn't lying," Keith said, concern now in his deep voice and pale eyes. "I've really never been to your town."

"You're going to wish you'd gone there earlier," Chance murmured.

"Why?" Keith asked impatiently. "What's in Forest Glen?"

Her name burned in his throat, so that he had to swallow before saying it. "Jessie Phillips."

Keith sucked in a breath of surprise. "Jessie?"

"So you remember who she is?" Not that Chance believed anyone could forget the beauty and spirit that was Jessie Phillips.

The man rubbed a slightly trembling hand over his face. "You never forget your first love."

"What about your second?" Chance asked.

"What?" Keith's brow furrowed again in confusion.

"Did you ever get married?" From his investigation, he knew the man lived alone now.

Keith narrowed his eyes and studied Chance. "That's a kind of personal question for a sheriff to ask me. What's this about? Why are you here?"

"It is personal," Chance admitted.

"Are you asking about me for Jessie?" Keith asked, almost hopefully.

"Answer my questions, and I'll explain why I'm here," Chance said. "Have you ever been married?"

"No." Keith sighed. "I tell people that I'm still too young to settle down. Only twenty-six. But I think I never really got over Jessie. The one that got away and all that."

"You dumped her," Chance said, reminding the man and himself that Keith had been a fool.

"I was eighteen and such an idiot," he admitted. "So she lives in Forest Glen?"

Chance had already told him as much, but the admission hadn't come easily. He wasn't entirely comfortable with this man knowing where she was. "Yes."

Keith chuckled again, with irony. "She's been living that close but I never found her."

"You've looked for her?"

The man grinned now. "Yeah. You must know her, probably pretty well since you know I was the idiot who broke up with her."

Chance nodded.

"Then you have to understand why I looked for her—once I grew up a little and realized what a jerk I'd been." Keith shook his head in self-disgust. "And how lucky I'd been that she'd ever loved a schmuck like me."

Chance had to nod again. "I don't know what she was

like back when you two knew each other," he allowed, "but she's pretty amazing now."

The guy scrutinized Chance more closely. "Are you and she involved?"

Their lovemaking flashed through Chance's mind, and tension filled his body. But that one night was all they'd had. With the possibility that he might be moving back to Chicago, he couldn't get any more involved with Jessie—and Tommy—than he already was.

"We're friends," Chance replied after some silent deliberation. "Just friends."

"Did she want you to find me?" Keith asked excitedly, his eyes bright.

Chance nodded. But she hadn't been the first one to ask him. He'd assured her that he wouldn't tell Keith Howard about Tommy—if he happened to run into the guy. Jessie wanted to tell him about his son herself.

"And she wanted you to talk to my friends and coworkers and check me out before she met with me again?" Keith asked.

"I thought it would be a good idea to check you out," he said. "People can change a lot in eight years." Robyn had changed a lot throughout their marriage, even before he'd deployed the first time.

"I thought Jessie hated me," Keith said, "after the cowardly way I dumped her."

"A letter was pretty cowardly," Chance agreed.

Keith's eyes widened in surprise. "You must be really good friends with her since you know about that stupid letter." He shook his head. "I was an idiot back then, such an idiot that I don't understand why she would even want to find me." He sucked in another breath as realization glimmered in his bright eyes. "I have a child, don't I?"

Dread knotted the muscles in Chance's stomach again. He shouldn't have talked to the man; it wasn't his place to tell Keith Howard he was a daddy. "You really need to talk to Jessie."

Keith uttered a ragged sigh. "I knew it. I knew she lied about being pregnant."

"But you never called her on it. Instead, you sent her that Dear Jane letter." Maybe Keith Howard wasn't the nice guy everyone claimed he was.

"I guess I didn't really want to know," Keith admitted. "I was a kid. I'd just left for college."

"And Jessie was only seventeen and all alone," Chance angrily informed the man.

"She wasn't alone," Keith insisted. "Her parents probably weren't happy with her for getting pregnant, but they would have been there for her."

"Maybe they would have if she'd moved to Germany with them when they retired." Now he understood why she hadn't; she'd needed their support, not their disapproval. "Instead she moved to Forest Glen and lived with an aunt and a cousin."

Keith dropped into a chair in front of the tall windows looking onto the street. "I was such a selfish jerk."

"She thinks she's the one who was selfish," Chance admitted.

"Why? Because she lied? That was selfless, not selfish." Keith defended the woman who'd kept him from his son. "I know she did it for me. She didn't want me to give up college and move back home."

Not unless he did it out of love. She deserved that, someone who would put her first always. No matter how much he wished otherwise, Chance couldn't be that guy.

"You're not mad," he mused as he studied Keith.

"Pissed as hell," he corrected Chance, "at myself for being a coward. I should have checked back, should have called her on her lie. She was a terrible liar."

"I can't imagine her ever lying," Chance agreed. But he had to remember that she had, and that he really shouldn't trust her.

"So what do I have? A son or a daughter?"

"Jessie should be the one who tells you about…" Her amazing kid.

"Okay." His head bobbed in agreement. "You're right. I need to talk to Jessie. Tell me about her. Is she married? Does she have any other kids?"

"She never married, either."

Hope lit up Keith's face with a wide grin. "Do you think…is it possible that she might still have feelings for me?"

The thought hadn't occurred to Chance…until now. Jealousy soured his stomach. "I think she was too busy to get involved with anyone because she's built her entire life around raising your child."

Keith nodded. "She's that kind of woman. Selfless. Generous."

"She's been worried that you'd be mad at her." Chance laughed, finally seeing the irony in the situation. "And you're actually still in love with her."

Keith didn't deny it. Instead he sighed. "Jessie Phillips is not the kind of woman a man ever really gets over."

That was Chance's second-greatest fear. His first was that he'd fallen for her. His second was that he would never get over her.

"So HOW did it go?" Jessie asked the minute she walked into Chance's office. Ever since he'd called to let her know he was back, she'd been a wreck. Instead of meeting later, as they'd planned, she'd asked Dr. Malewitz and Ruth if she could leave work early. The minute they'd agreed—a knowing, matchmaking look passing between them—she had headed right over to the sheriff's office.

Chance glanced up from his computer, his eyes darkening as he met her gaze. Then he stood up and came around the desk. But he didn't reach for her and pull her into his arms like she longed for him to do. Instead he just stood there, close enough that she felt his warmth. Heat flooded her, too, and she knew it wasn't just news of Keith she'd rushed over to hear. She'd wanted to see Chance. She'd missed him, so much that she lifted her hand, as if to touch his face, and her fingers trembled.

She'd been a wreck since he'd called an hour ago. She'd been a wreck since Chance had admitted he'd found Keith. But her nerves had actually first kicked in when he'd carried her up to his bed and she'd finally stopped fighting her feelings for him. Those emotions rushed over her again as her heart pounded and her pulse raced.

She longed to throw her arms around his neck and press her lips to his. But she resisted and pulled her hand back to her side. Her feelings didn't matter now. All that mattered was Tommy. "So it was really him?"

Chance nodded. "His date of birth and social security number matched the kid you'd gone to high school with. I knew it was him before I even went to Battle Creek," he reminded her.

"I know. I know. It just seems strange that he was

so close all this time…" She forced back her nerves. "I never figured he'd move to Michigan."

"He went to college here," he pointed out. "Is that why you moved here, because you knew he was close and you wanted to be close to him?"

She studied his handsome face, trying to determine if she had detected a note of jealousy in his voice. "I had no place else to go," she said. "The only family I had left was my aunt and cousin here."

"So you didn't think about him at all?" he asked, as if he was interrogating her.

She sighed as she remembered her youthful optimism. "No. I've thought about him every day."

Chance sucked in a breath, confirming that he was jealous despite his reluctance to get involved any deeper with her.

"In the beginning, I thought he would find me and tell me that he couldn't live without me," she said, admitting to her youthful idealism. "And when I stopped waiting for him to come sweep me off my feet, I started worrying that he would find me and take Tommy away from me." And that fear had just increased when Chance had told her that he'd found him. "So yeah, I think about him every day."

"I'm sorry," he said with a heavy sigh. "I had no right to question you. It's not any of my business."

"I made it your business," she reminded him, "when I asked you to find him for me."

"For you or for Tommy?" He pushed his hand through his dark hair, disheveling the silky soft strands. "Forget I asked that."

"Do you care?" she wondered, although she suspected that he did. It didn't matter, though. She'd given up long ago on Keith or any other man sweeping her off her feet. But that night Chance had carried her up the stairs had reminded her of that youthful, romantic dream.

"I don't have the right to care," he replied. "My chances of winning the custody battle for Matthew are slim to none. And if I don't win, I'll move back to Chicago to be close to him."

Ignoring the pain clenching her heart, she nodded. "Of course. Matthew has to come first. Like Tommy comes first for me. I wanted you to find Keith for him. Not me."

"I didn't have the right to ask," he repeated. "But I'm glad you told me." He stepped closer, so that his chest brushed against hers. His heart pounded just as hard, if not harder, than hers.

He wanted her. She saw the desire in his gaze as he stared down at her. But they were in his office, with Eleanor sitting at the desk outside the open door. Jessie didn't care that people talked about them except that she was scared Tommy had heard some of it, and that was why he'd started wanting Chance as his father instead of Keith.

"So you talked to people about Keith." She steered the conversation back to Tommy's dad. "What did they say about him?"

"Only positive things," he said.

"That's good, then."

He nodded. "I talked to him, too."

"You did?"

"I had to know...for myself...that it would be safe to tell him where you and Tommy are."

"You didn't tell him about Tommy."

"I didn't have to," Chance said. "He already knew."

"You told him." She should have been mad that he'd interfered, but she was actually relieved that he'd done the hardest thing for her.

A bell dinged above the door to the street, announcing someone's arrival. A deep voice rumbled in conversation with Eleanor. She ignored it all as she waited for Chance's explanation. All he offered was, "He says he kind of always knew."

"But he didn't look for us," she said.

"He tried." Chance defended the man. "You weren't easy to find."

"I wasn't hiding."

"I couldn't find you." Keith Howard walked into the office. He had the same wiry build he'd had as a teenager. His hair was a chocolate brown and only slightly shorter than he used to wear it. And his pale blue eyes twinkled with the humor and intelligence she remembered him having and that she'd noticed her son—their son—possessed.

"Let me give you two some privacy," Chance offered. He passed Keith in the doorway and pulled the door closed on his way out.

Jessie stared after him, just barely restraining the urge to call him back. She needed him at her side. She just needed him.

Keith looked exactly like the boy she'd once loved. But she didn't love the boy anymore. She loved the man that was Sheriff Chance Drayton.

"So you found my dad?" Tommy asked the sheriff, who'd picked him up from school. The principal had called him out of class early, as if it were a doctor or dentist appointment. Or worse, as if something had happened to his mom. But Chance had assured him it wasn't anything bad.

Tommy wasn't convinced. He wished Chance had just picked him up because he'd missed him. The way he'd touched his hair, and the way he'd smiled, he'd acted almost like he had with Matthew, all proud and loving.

"Yeah, I found your dad," Chance replied as he opened the passenger door for Tommy. "He's in my office with your mom. That's where I'm taking you so you can meet him."

"I wish you hadn't found him," Tommy admitted. "I wish I'd never asked you to find him."

"He's a really nice guy," Chance promised. "You'll like him."

Tommy doubted it. No matter how nice he was, he wasn't Chance. "Is he alone?"

The sheriff nodded.

"He doesn't have a wife or a bunch of little kids?" He had to know.

"Nope."

So he had no younger brothers or sisters. No family.

"You'll like him," Chance said, taking his hand off the wheel to gently squeeze Tommy's shoulder. "You two have the same eyes. And he laughs and smiles a lot. He's really excited to meet you."

"Oh."

"Tommy, this is what you wanted," Chance reminded him. "You wanted to find your real dad."

"I don't want that anymore," Tommy admitted.

"What do you want?"

"You." He decided to share his new dreams. "I want you to be my dad and Matt to be my brother and for all of us to be a family."

Chance's breath made a loud noise. "I'm sorry."

"Why? It can still happen. It doesn't matter that you found my dad."

"No, it doesn't," Chance said. "It doesn't make any difference because I probably can't stay in Forest Glen. I'll have to move back to Chicago to be part of Matt's life."

"What about mine?" he asked, hating that his voice got almost as squeaky as Christopher Johnson's. "What about Mom's? Don't you want to be part of our lives?"

"Tommy..."

He was such a stupid little kid. He might as well write Santa Claus a letter or put a tooth under his pillow. He'd stopped believing in those fairy tales a long time ago—at least a couple of years. But they were more real than his chances of ever having the family he wanted. He saw that now.

That time he'd spent with Chance building the tree house and playing catch, and the time he'd played with Matt and slept in the tree house, and when all of them ate dinner together. That had been like watching a movie—really fun while it lasted, but then it was over.

He turned away from Chance and stared out the window and sucked up his tears. He wouldn't cry. Tommy Phillips wasn't a baby anymore.

Chapter Thirteen

"I feel like such a creep," Chance said.

"Yeah, suing for full custody was a mistake," Trenton agreed. "So it was really big of Robyn to offer to compromise with you."

Chance glanced at his friend, who sat in a chair next to him, his designer shoes propped up on the porch railing. "I wasn't talking about the custody battle."

"No?" Trenton lifted the bottle of beer to his lips and swallowed hard. "Then why'd you call me to come up here again?"

"I didn't call you as my lawyer," Chance admitted. "I called you as my friend." They'd known each other a long time and had been competitors as well as friends, so the admission was an unusual, and uncomfortable, one for Chance to make.

Shocked, Trenton dropped his feet onto the floor and turned toward him. "What's going on?"

"I told you. I feel like a creep. I started something with Jessie Phillips and I let her son believe that something was possible that isn't possible." He sighed with self-disgust. "Hell, I let myself believe it—that I could make a life here, that I could make this house a home and live in it with my family."

"You're not talking about just Matthew. You're talking about the Phillipses, too." Trenton sighed now.

"I never had a chance, did I?"

"With Jessie Phillips?" Trenton shrugged. "I don't know. I just saw you two in the car that one time. It looked pretty intense."

"You don't know the half of it." He'd never felt passion or pleasure as powerfully as he had the night he made love with Jessie. "But I mean the custody case. I never had a chance, did I?" This was the conversation he'd had to have in person, so he could see as well as hear the answer.

"Are you asking your lawyer or your friend?" Trenton wanted to know.

"Both."

Resignation and sympathy softened the lawyer's usually hard gaze. "Robyn's a good mom. No judge would take her son away from her and award you full custody, no matter how good a dad—or a man—you are."

"And I'm a creep." He'd been calling himself that pretty much since he'd kept his promise to Tommy Phillips when he'd found Keith Howard three weeks ago. He'd kept his promise but broken the kid's heart. And he would never forgive himself for causing Tommy pain.

"Chance—"

"Don't defend me."

"That's what you're paying me for," Trenton said. "That's why I tried to do my best for you in the custody case."

"Even though you knew you couldn't win it. You were willing to break your record for me?" Guilt at taking out his frustration on Trenton made Chance feel ashamed.

"I was willing to hope I was wrong," Trenton said.

"To be fair, you warned me," Chance said. "About the custody case."

Swigging the beer again, his friend just offered another nod.

"And Jessie Phillips," Chance added. "You knew I shouldn't get involved with anyone."

"Because I know you want a relationship with Matthew," Trenton explained. "He's the most important person to you, more important than yourself."

"And the only way I'll probably get that relationship with my son is to agree to the joint custody offer and move back to Chicago."

"You can get your old job back on the force," Trenton assured him. "Hell, I know they miss you. You were a damn good detective, so good that you must be bored out of your mind here."

Chance smiled. "I'm not bored."

"That's right. You got hurt more here than you ever did in Chicago or Afghanistan."

And he was afraid that he'd inflicted more hurt than he'd received. "I have to give my notice here, give them time to find another sheriff, before I can move back to Chicago. That might take a month or so."

"Yeah, who'd be willing to move here?" Trenton shuddered at the thought. Yet he kept coming back.

Chance laughed, unconvinced that the small town hadn't already grown on his big city lawyer. "You might find this place is a whole lot more exciting than you think."

"You only find it exciting because of that gorgeous redhead," Trenton said. "If she wasn't here, you probably would have been bored out of your mind."

Chance shook his head. "No. I love this town. I still think it would be the perfect place to raise my son."

"You'll never convince Robyn of that."

"I know."

"But her lawyer and I might be able to talk her into allowing Matthew another visit before you move back to Chicago. The kid loved it here. And school will be out for the summer next month."

"I'm not sure that's a good idea," Chance admitted. Having his son here would only torture Chance even more with what might have been.

"Don't you need that closure—the two of you?" Trenton asked, reminding Chance that the man had dated a shrink for a while. "Maybe his next visit will suck so much that you'll both be glad to move back to Chicago."

Since Keith Howard spent so much time with Jessie and Tommy now, Matthew's visit wouldn't be the same as it had been last time. It wouldn't feel as if they'd formed their own family. He still had the tree house, bunk beds and the dog. But Chance had a feeling that, like him, his son would miss the Phillipses the most when they moved back to Chicago.

"He's GOING to move here," Jessie told Belinda, her hand shaking so much as she poured the wine that the red liquid sloshed over the rim of her cousin's glass.

"He's already living here," Belinda said as she sopped up the mess with a napkin. "And he's a shoo-in for the election this fall."

"I'm not talking about Chance." It was bad enough that all she did—day and night—was think about him. "I'm talking about Tommy's dad."

Belinda lifted a dark blond brow. "Keith is uprooting his whole life in Battle Creek?"

"He's selling his condo and quitting his job to become a tax accountant here," she replied.

Her cousin nodded. "So yeah, he's uprooting his whole life. The question is, is he doing it for his son—" she arched her brow again "—or for you?"

Jessie sighed with regret. "I think for me."

Instead of being angry with her, as she'd expected and probably deserved, Keith had been apologetic and considerate and determined to make up for all the years he'd missed with his son. And with her.

With a laugh, Belinda teased, "Quit monopolizing all the single men in Forest Glen. First you stake your claim on the sheriff and now on Keith."

"I haven't staked my claim on anyone," Jessie insisted although she wished she could have.

"Keeping your options open." Belinda winked and nodded her approval. "Smart."

"If only I had options…" But Chance had backed off, ostensibly to give Tommy time to get to know his real dad. But why hadn't he called *her?* Why hadn't he come over to see *her?*

"So you've made your decision?" Belinda asked, leaning forward with interest.

Jessie shook her head. "I have no decisions to make."

"Not yet. But with Keith moving here, I bet you're going to have a decision to make soon—when he proposes."

Jessie laughed.

"You think that's funny?"

"It's ironic that when I wanted him to propose, he was

nowhere around, and now…" When she wanted another man to propose, Keith might.

"You did love him once," Belinda said, probably remembering all those tears she'd mopped up when Jessie had first come to live with her and her mom. "Are any of those old feelings still there?"

"I don't know," she answered honestly. Keith had grown from a smart, funny boy into a man determined to take responsibility. While it would make sense for Tommy—and the family he wanted—for her to rekindle her old feelings for Keith, she was too preoccupied with new feelings for Chance.

"Where's Tommy tonight?" Belinda asked with a glance around the quiet, tidy house. "Spending the night with his dad?"

Jessie shook her head. "Keith asked him." He'd even tried to bribe him with a trip to the Binder Park Zoo, but their son had apparently forgotten his love of animals and informed his parents he'd already seen it and didn't care to return. "But Tommy's not ready to spend time alone with the father he just met."

"It didn't take him long with the sheriff," Belinda said. "In fact, Tommy took to that man like Chance Drayton was his daddy."

Jessie sighed. "I know."

"You took to that man, too."

"It doesn't matter. Our lives are too complicated right now."

"So?" Belinda challenged her. "When isn't life complicated? Stuff always comes up. A cute teller at the bank your husband manages, and suddenly you're single again." She grinned despite the pain she'd suffered over her ex-husband's betrayal. "There are no guarantees, Jess. You need to take your happiness when and where you can."

She'd done that—that incredible time she and Chance had made love. "It's impossible."

"Why? Tommy's not here. Is he spending the night at the Johnsons?"

Jessie nodded.

"So call Chance." Without waiting for her agreement, Belinda picked up the cordless phone and lightly tossed it to Jessie. "Call him!"

"I will," she promised. "After you leave."

Belinda shook her head and crossed her arms over her chest. "I don't trust you. I want to hear the call."

Knowing her cousin's stubbornness, Jessie picked up the phone and punched in the numbers with a trembling hand. He picked up on the first ring, his deep voice a sexy rumble as he identified himself, "Sheriff Drayton."

"H-hi," she stammered.

His breath audibly caught. "Jessie?"

"Yes."

"Is everything all right?"

She smiled at his instant concern. "You're always the sheriff. Yes, everything's all right.

Belinda mouthed, "No, it's not."

Her cousin was right. "But I wondered if we could talk."

He hesitated a long moment before uttering his answer in a sexy rasp. "Yes."

"I'll come over there, then," she offered and clicked off the connection before she lost her nerve.

"You did the right thing," Belinda encouraged her. "You deserve some time for you."

Too bad she already knew that it wouldn't last.

THE KNOCK AT THE DOOR bumped Chance's pulse into overdrive. It had been racing since her call. They were going to talk—just talk. Chance had to tell her that he'd given his notice to the mayor and that he was leaving for Chicago as soon as his replacement was found.

But before he said anything, he just needed to see her. To touch her…

His body tense with anticipation, he pulled open the door—to Tommy's dad. "Oh…"

"I take it I'm not who you were expecting," Keith said with that ready grin and sparkle of good humor that made it impossible for anyone to hate the guy, no matter how much Chance wished he could.

"No, I wasn't expecting you." Was Jessie? Had she arranged for both of them to meet with Chance?

"Don't worry," Keith assured him. "I'll get out of your way…if I can have just a couple minutes of your time."

Chance stepped back so Keith could join him in the foyer. Then he closed the door. "Sure. Do you need my service or my protection?"

The younger man sighed. "I appreciate your finding me and checking me out for Jessie…"

"But?"

"I don't need anything else from you in a professional way."

Chance's head pounded with confusion. "I don't understand…"

"I need you to step aside."

Somehow Chance suspected he wasn't talking about giving him more room in the foyer, but he asked for clarification anyways. "What do you mean?"

"You told me, when we met in Battle Creek, that you're just Jessie's friend," Keith reminded him.

"Yes, I did."

"But it seems like there's more going on between you. At least Tommy thinks there is. And because of that, he's not really giving me a chance." No humor glinted in the man's eyes now, only frustration and sadness that Chance knew all too well.

"I'm sorry," he said. "Do you want me to talk to him about it?"

Keith shook his head. "No. In fact, I'd like you to do just the opposite. I'd like you to back off and give me some time to bond with my son."

Chance's temper kicked in along with his jealousy. "Back off? What the hell do you think I've been doing? I haven't seen Jessie or Tommy since the first day you came to town." And it had been killing him to stay away the past month.

"I didn't realize that." Keith grimaced. "It's just that Tommy talks about you so much. Chance this. Chance that. I jumped to conclusions. I'm really sorry. I hope you can overlook my being an ass."

"You're not being an ass," Chance assured him. "You're a father who just wants a relationship with his son."

"You understand?"

"I'm a father who wants a relationship with my son," he commiserated. "And that's not easy to manage when you don't live together."

"I want to change that," Keith said.

"You want to move in with Jessie?"

"I want to marry her."

"You've proposed?" Was that what she wanted to talk to Chance about? Did she want his blessing?

"Not yet," Keith said. "But I intend to. She's the same sweet girl I loved back in high school."

"I wouldn't count on that," Chance advised. "She's raised a child alone. She's changed. She's stronger. More independent than that seventeen-year-old you knew so long ago."

"You sound like you know her well, but you haven't lived in Forest Glen very long."

"Like I said, she's my friend." And hopefully she would remain his friend when he told her he was leaving.

"I want to be more than her friend," Keith reiterated.

Chance's head pounded harder with the thought of Jessie in a relationship, married to this man with whom she shared a child. He should be happy for her, should be happy for them all. But, selfishly, he couldn't imagine her with anyone but him.

"I'm not going to stand in your way," Chance assured the other man. He had no right to do that.

"You could," Keith said, "if you wanted. Tommy isn't the only one who talks about you. Jessie does, too, and with a certain look on her face…" He released a ragged sigh of frustration. "It reminds me of the way she used to look at me."

Chance's pulse quickened again. But it didn't really matter because he wasn't sticking around. He could have shared that with Keith to allay his fears, but he needed to tell Jessie first.

"You must think I'm a jerk," Keith said. "After all, I'm the one who broke up with her. But I was so young and stupid and thought having a girl back home would mess up my whole college experience. It didn't take me long to figure out that I wasn't going to find anyone better than Jess. But she was gone by the time I finally got smart and tried to contact her. And I couldn't find her."

Having already heard this story when they'd met in Battle Creek, Chance only nodded.

Keith sighed with self-disgust. "I'm sorry to go on—it's just that I have so much to make up for. I want to give my son the family he should have had. I want to marry his mother, like I would have had I known for certain that she was pregnant. I just want…"

It was everything Chance wanted for himself. "I understand."

"Thank you for listening to me." Keith held out his hand.

Chance studied it for a moment before he shook. He couldn't offer any words of encouragement or luck, though. It would probably be best for Tommy if his parents married, but only if Jessie cared about Keith the way he cared about her. She deserved happiness, too.

"Well, I've taken enough of your time," Keith said. "And I can tell you're expecting someone, so I'll get out of your way."

Chance nodded in acknowledgment that he was waiting for someone, but he didn't offer the identity of his visitor. He just pulled open the door and hoped Jessie wasn't standing out on the porch.

When he closed the door behind Keith Howard, Chance leaned back against the solid oak. His breath shuddered out of his lungs as emotions warred within him. Guilt battled jealousy, anticipation and regret.

A fist hammered the door behind him, rattling the wood. Maybe Keith had run into Jessie and returned to angrily confront him. Welcoming a fight and a satisfying physical release for his roiling emotions, he jerked open the door.

To Jessie's beautiful face, flushed with emotions of her own. "Chance." She breathed his name on a wistful sigh, her eyes bright.

"I'm glad you're here," he said, although that was a hell of an understatement. He was ecstatic that she was there, but he couldn't enjoy her closeness until he told her that he would be leaving soon. "We really need to talk."

"Talk?" she asked, her voice a challenge that had Chance's nerves tingling. She stepped into the foyer and closed the door behind her.

"Yeah," he replied. "That's why you wanted to come over here. That's what you said when you called."

"That's what I said," she agreed, fiddling with the belt of her raincoat.

He glanced out the window of the door, but sunlight glimmered through the glass. As summer drew closer, the days grew longer and brighter and warmer. "You don't need that raincoat," he said, narrowing his eyes to study her.

"You're right," she said, and she pulled the belt free of its loops, then shrugged the coat off her shoulders. The tan material dropped down and pooled around the high, skinny heels she had on. Those heels were all she wore as she stood naked before him.

A groan slipped involuntarily from his throat. "No, you don't need the coat…"

"I just need you," she said, her hands sliding up his chest to link behind his neck.

His body tensed as her soft, naked curves pressed against him. He ached for her, ached to make love to her as passionately as they had a month ago.

"I need to talk." He had so much to tell her, so much he needed to tell her, but he couldn't think—not with her so tantalizingly close.

She rose on tiptoe and skimmed her lips along his jaw. "I don't want to talk." She arched her back, pressing her breasts against his chest so he could feel the tautness of her nipples. "I just want *you*."

His control snapped, and he took her mouth with his in a kiss full of the passion burning inside him. For her. He swung her up in his arms and carried her up the stairs. Nearly drunk with desire, he stumbled.

She laughed, her giggle tickling his lips. Her hands were busy, too, pulling his buttons free so she could push off his shirt. When she reached for his belt, he stopped in the hall. And he lifted her higher, so that his lips could skim down the slender arch of her throat, over the slope of first one breast and then the other. His lips tugged at a nipple. Then he suckled her.

She pulled his belt free then unsnapped his jeans. And she dipped her fingers inside the waistband of both the jeans and the briefs he wore underneath. As she stroked the tip of his erection, he shuddered. He couldn't make it to the bedroom, no matter that it was only a few doors down the hall.

Instead he laid her on the carpet running the length of the hall, and he made love to her with his mouth, stroking his tongue in and out of her moist heat. Her nails dug into his shoulders as she screamed his name.

He pulled a condom from his wallet, then dropped his jeans and briefs onto the floor. She took the foil pocket from his hands, ripped it open with her teeth, then rolled the latex down the length of his pulsing erection. Out of his mind with desire, Chance lifted her legs and thrust inside her. She arched, and he realized she lay on the hard floor. He turned, putting his own back against the carpet as she straddled him.

His hands on the sweet curve of her hips, he helped her find her rhythm. And every time she moved, he thrust up. She came, screaming his name. And he followed her into mind-blowing ecstasy.

But he hadn't entirely lost his senses. Because he realized what he'd done. He'd fallen in love with Jessie Phillips.

Chapter Fourteen

Laughter flowed with the sunshine through the trees and across the grass of Forest Glen's park. The first week of summer vacation had brought everyone out to enjoy the warm weather and freedom. Sitting alone on a bench, Jessie watched everybody else playing. Tommy and Keith twirled a Frisbee across the grass between them, while Chance and Matthew tossed a baseball back and forth in a serious game of catch.

He hadn't called her since that day and night of passion and madness at his house, in his bed, three weeks ago. She shouldn't have listened to Belinda. The raincoat had been a cliché, however effective. But their lovemaking hadn't brought the simple happiness she'd thought it would; instead, it had left her with more heartache because she'd only fallen more deeply in love with Chance.

He hadn't fallen for her, though. Because if he had, he wouldn't be leaving. He hadn't told her he was, because she hadn't let him say the words, but she'd seen it in his eyes. The goodbye he wanted to tell her. Instead, he'd given Keith an endorsement—said that he'd be a good dad if Tommy would let him.

It was her fault that Tommy paid more attention to

Chance and Matthew than to his father. She'd robbed them of the relationship they would have had, stealing so many years from them with her selfishness and fear. Just like Robyn was robbing Chance and Matthew of their relationship. Like Tommy, she couldn't keep her gaze from that father and son.

Love and pride radiated from Chance to Matthew. He loved his boy so much that he would do anything to be with him. That was why she knew he was leaving. He must have realized, as she had, that he would not be awarded full custody, no matter how much he was willing to give up for his son.

The puppy frolicked between the boys, bouncing back and forth. Other townspeople gathered around. Mrs. Wilson had a cat on a leash, which Chance, grinning, steered clear of. Mrs. Applegate, a parasol over her shoulder to shield her pale complexion from the sun, flirted with Chance and the blond man who joined him on the grass. The lawyer, in his expensive tailored suit, looked more out of place than the cat on the leash.

She pulled her camera from the bag sitting beside her on the bench. Clicking the Record button, she mentally directed her own film of Forest Glen, catching scenes from different areas of the park. The older women in the rose garden. The toddlers in the sandbox. The bigger kids playing on the equipment, smaller ones bobbing back and forth on spring animals. But there was a definite star of her video: Chance. And in supporting roles, Matthew and Tommy.

She only lowered the camera when a shadow fell across her, and she noticed the battery light blinking its low power warning. Glancing up, she was surprised to meet the steady gaze of Chance's lawyer. "Hello?"

"Jessie, right?"

She nodded.

He held out a hand. "Trenton Sanders."

She closed her fingers around his, and he surprised her again with the calluses she felt. He didn't seem the type to work with his hands; she would have figured he relied mostly on his charm and brains. "It's nice to meet you."

"If that little old lady hadn't latched on to Chance, he probably would have tackled me before I made it over here," he said.

She glanced away to see Mrs. Applegate clutching Chance's arm, her parasol bumping against his shoulder and chin. Hopefully he wouldn't lose an eye on the spiky point. "So he doesn't want you talking to me?"

He shook his head but not a lock of moussed blond hair fell out of place, despite the wind blowing through it. "No. He'd rather I stayed far away from you."

"He said that?"

"Chance doesn't say much," Trenton admitted.

She really should have let Chance talk when he'd wanted to. But her body still hummed with the pleasure he'd given her and she had no regrets. No matter how hard it would be for her to get over him, she had no regrets.

"He doesn't need to say much for people to like him." She gestured toward the townspeople gathered around him and Matthew.

"I think you more than like him," Trenton said as he settled onto the bench next to her.

"I care about Chance," she admitted, glancing down at the camera in her hands. She fiddled with the latch to the memory card.

"Then you're not going to be like all those people ganging up on him and trying to talk him out of doing what he needs to do? He's miserable without his son. He has to have Matthew in his life."

"I know."

"That's who got him out of Afghanistan. He'd made a promise to Matthew to come back in one piece, safe and sound. And he made damn sure he kept that promise."

"Then why did he go back the second time?" He'd only told her that he had to.

"We'd met another little kid, a boy who reminded us both of Matthew." He stopped and swallowed hard. "And Chance had made a promise to that kid, too."

"You were there?" she asked.

He nodded. "Just the first time. I didn't go back."

"But Chance did. Because of this boy you'd met?"

He nodded again. "The kid was sick. Chance promised him he'd come back and help him. He wanted to get him to a medical center to see if he could have him flown back to the States for the surgery he needed."

"And did he?"

Trenton shook his head. "No. By the time he was debriefed and sent back, the boy had died."

Jessie blinked away the sting of tears but couldn't keep her voice from cracking. "That's so sad."

"What's sadder is that he lost two boys then. His signing up for another tour violated his custody arrangement with Robyn, and she successfully filed for full custody of Matthew."

"That's horrible," she said, her heart aching for the loss Chance had suffered.

"Yeah, it is."

"Why didn't you help him?" she asked.

"He didn't ask me then. I got hurt on our first tour, would have died if not for Chance. So I didn't go back with him. I was recovering and getting my practice going again. Maybe that was why he didn't tell me. Maybe he figured she'd change her mind when he came back. I didn't know what was going on until it was over. So we had to wait until he returned to petition the court to reconsider that decision and award full custody to Chance."

"But you never really believed you could win?" she realized. The man was too smart for that.

"I thought it might get Robyn and Chance talking again."

"You were trying to get them back together?"

He sighed. "That's why I don't play matchmaker. My plan totally backfired. They hate each other even more than they did before."

She glanced at Keith, grateful he didn't hate her as she'd feared. "Why can't Robyn see why he had to go back? She's a doctor."

"She was his wife first."

"She's still a mother. She needs to think about Matthew and what's best for him." Like Jessie needed to think about Tommy and what was best for him. She couldn't put her own fears or hopes and desires before him again. Her fingers trembling, she opened the slot and popped out the memory card. Then she handed it over to Trenton. "Give her this," she said. "Maybe she'll understand."

Trenton stared down at the card and then lifted his gaze to hers. "I do now. I understand what Chance sees in you. I knew it wasn't just the beauty or the passion. He's not the kind of guy who's ever cared much about looks or sex appeal. He cares about substance. You've got that."

"Yeah, I've got that." But it was not enough to let her keep the man she loved.

CHANCE DRAGGED his hand from his pocket, fisted it and pounded on Jessie's front door. He'd put this off long enough. He had to tell her before he made the official announcement at the next town council meeting; he owed her that much and more.

After the nastiness of his divorce, he had doubted he would ever be able to love again. But not only had he fallen for Jessie, he'd fallen harder than he ever had. He was no longer the idealistic fool who'd married Robyn with thoughts of conquering the world and living happily ever after. He loved Jessie, but he'd learned the hard way that happily ever after wasn't always possible, and a man could live a long time on perfect, happy moments.

He lifted his hand to knock again just as the door drew open. His fist nearly connected with Keith Howard's smiling face. Keith laughed, but the humor didn't entirely reach his eyes. "Sheriff, what brings you by?" He sounded possessive as if he'd already moved in and was defending his own.

Maybe he had moved in. The possibility churned Chance's stomach. But before he could reply, Jessie shouldered her ex-boyfriend out of the way. "Keith, Tommy's packing his things for the overnighter. Can you help him?"

He hesitated, as if he intended to stay and witness their discussion. But Jessie glared until he turned tail and left them alone. Instead of welcoming him inside the house, though, she stepped outside and joined him

on the porch. "Sorry about that," she murmured. "He...
he wants..."

"You."

She sighed. "He thinks I'm still that young girl who
was besotted with him. He doesn't realize that I've
changed—that I don't want what I did back then."

"Him?"

She nodded. And the heat in her eyes told him who
she desired. Chance. But she didn't say the words this
time.

"He's trying to make up for the years he missed with
you and Tommy," Chance said. "He wants you to be a
family."

Jessie nodded. "I know. He thinks it's what would be
best for Tommy."

"He's probably right."

"Is that why you're going home to Chicago? You're
going back to Robyn."

He laughed. "I'm not sure what's funnier—the fact
that you think that Robyn would actually take me back
or the fact that you already know I'm leaving."

"I've known for a while," she admitted.

"Before Trenton talked to you in the park last
weekend?" he asked, reliving the jealousy he'd felt as
he'd watched his friend share that narrow bench with
Jessie.

She laughed now. "Yes."

"So he was just flirting with you?" Trenton had
thought she was hot the first time he'd seen her. And
the slick lawyer possessed a charm, in and out of the
courtroom, that Chance had never had.

She shook her head. "I don't think I'm his type."

"Then he's crazier than I thought," Chance murmured.

"Almost as crazy as I am." For leaving her. "I should have known that you would have already heard. There are no secrets in this town."

She sighed. "No, there aren't. Except…when are you leaving?"

"Soon. The mayor found a replacement for me who can start next week." And his mother had threatened to find a replacement for the mayor because of it. She'd even offered to back Trenton if he would move to Forest Glen and run for office. He hadn't seen his friend that horrified since their tour in Afghanistan. "We're going to make an announcement at the town council meeting tonight."

"I'm glad you came by—because I wasn't planning on attending."

He glanced at the house. "Right. You have company—you wouldn't want to leave."

"No. They're on their way out. Tommy agreed to spend the night with Keith at his new place. He's renting a little house Dr. Malewitz and his wife own in town."

He was just renting, probably because he planned on moving in with Jessie and Tommy soon. Chance couldn't fault the guy for trying to win her back. But he was damn glad he wouldn't be around to witness his inevitable success. Jessie would do what she thought best for her son.

She smiled grimly. "It's ironic really. He's moving to town and you're moving out."

"I'll hate to leave," he said, hoping she knew that was mostly because of her.

"But you have to do what's best for your son." The door creaked behind them as if someone was listening at it. She sighed. "We both do."

He nodded. "Taking Matthew away from his mother would have been the mistake you thought it was. It wouldn't have been the right thing for Matt. No matter how angry I am with Robyn, he needs his mother in his life."

"He needs his father, too," she assured him. Then she reached out with that generosity of spirit he loved most about her and hugged him. "I'm going to…" her voice cracked with emotion "…miss you."

Chance closed his arms around her, holding her close to his aching heart for several silent moments. Her silky hair brushed his cheek, and he breathed in the sweet, flowery essence of her—trying to commit her scent and feel to his memory so that he would never forget any detail about her. Leaving Matthew when he'd been deployed had been the hardest thing Chance had ever done. But this came close.

"You need to say goodbye to Tommy, too," she insisted, pulling away as if to call out to her son.

"I know," he said. The thought of telling the boy he was leaving filled Chance with dread. "But I don't want to mess up his fun night with his dad. I'll talk to him before I leave."

"What about me?" she asked, staring up at him, eyes damp with tears.

"I can't…see you again…and say goodbye…" He kissed her, a tender parting kiss that he'd feel forever on his lips and in his soul. Then he released her and turned and walked away.

"HAVE YOU changed your mind?" Keith—Dad—asked. "Do you want to go home now?"

"No." Because home wasn't that little house he'd

lived in as far back as he could remember. Home was Chance's yellow farmhouse with the bunk beds and the tree house in the big backyard. And Chance and Matt. But the sheriff was moving away, and he wasn't coming back.

Tommy had listened in on the conversation between Chance and his mom. He'd heard everything. And he'd seen them hug and kiss. How could they just give up on each other?

Tears burned his eyes like smoke from a bonfire. He squeezed them shut for a little bit. When he opened them up again, his dad crouched in front of the sofa where Tommy sat.

"What's wrong? Tell me, and I'll try to make it better." Keith—Dad's—eyes glistened as if he were going to cry, too, and his voice was all raspy. "Let me help you."

Tommy felt even more like crying because Keith was trying to be all loving and nice. He was trying to be the dad Tommy had wanted him to be before he'd met Chance. "You won't wanna help me with what I want to do," Tommy warned him. "Can I use the phone?"

"Who do you want to call? Who do you want to help you?" It looked as if his dad was holding his breath, scared of the name Tommy might give him.

"Matt."

Dad's forehead squeezed together like the ridges on a dipping potato chip. "Matthew? The sheriff's son?"

"My brother." He glanced down at his hand. The Band-Aid had fallen off a long time ago, but there was a little pink scar where he'd cut the skin.

"Brother?" Dad rubbed his forehead now, as if he

wanted to smooth out those lines. "You don't have a brother."

"I have a blood brother," Tommy insisted. And he lifted his pinkie.

Dad must have seen the scar because he nodded. "And this brother is Matthew?"

Tommy nodded. "I have to call him."

"Okay," his dad agreed. "He's gone back to Chicago, though."

"I have his number." He'd memorized it a long time ago. "He has a cell phone."

"Isn't he just ten?"

"Yeah, but his mom got him one when he came to visit Chance over spring break, so that he could call her if he wanted to go back to her apartment."

"Can I ask why you want to call Matt?"

Tommy sniffled back the tears that kept burning in his nose and the back of his throat. "He's gotta talk his mom into moving here like you. Then him and Chance can stay in Forest Glen. And we can be a family."

Dad's face got really pale, as if he had the flu or something. "Who can be a family?"

"Me and Mom and Matt and Chance." He didn't say it to be mean, but his dad looked as if he'd punched him in the face. "It's not like I don't like you."

"But you don't know me," he said. "But it took you a while to get to know Chance, too. You just have to give me time."

"It didn't take any time with Chance," Tommy explained. "I just walked into his office and asked him to find my dad."

"He did, Tommy. He found me."

"No, it's like he was my dad. He just felt like he was. And Matt feels like my brother."

"But he's not your dad. I am."

"I know—and I want to spend time with you," Tommy assured the guy. "I can spend the night and hang out. But I don't want to live with you."

"That's not really up to you to decide yet. You're not old enough."

Tommy sighed. "I know. I'm never old enough to understand. But sometimes I think I get it and nobody else does. Except for Matt. He gets that we're the family."

"That's up to your mother, son."

"She's really happy with Chance. Happy like I've never seen her. She smiles not just with her mouth but her eyes and her whole face. Doesn't Mom deserve to be happy? Why should she have to keep putting what's best for me before what's best for her?"

His dad's mouth dropped open. "Are you sure you're only eight?"

"I know. Right. I feel so much older."

"You're definitely wise, my boy."

Wise meant smart. Tommy knew that. But he couldn't figure out if his dad agreed with him. He just wiped his eyes and handed Tommy the cordless phone so he could call his brother. Tommy didn't even wait for Matt to say anything before he blurted, "We gotta do something to save our family!"

Chapter Fifteen

With a box in his hands, Chance headed toward the front door. Cookie snagged the leg of his jeans, playfully growling and snarling as she chewed on the denim around his ankle and tried to keep him from answering the knock at the door.

Or maybe she was trying to keep him from moving, like everyone else in Forest Glen. Except Jessie. She'd understood that he had to do this—for his son. No one had ever known him as completely as Jessie did. So she must also realize that he loved her even though he hadn't thought it fair to tell her.

Cookie barked and grabbed at Chance's jeans again, nipping some of his skin with the material.

"Hey, dog, you should be happy," he told the feisty pup. "You're going to live with Tommy Phillips when I move. You love it at his house. You love him." Chance loved him, too. He had yet to say goodbye to the little boy; he didn't know how he'd manage it.

Another knock rattled the door. Chance managed a smile. Trenton was always so damn impatient. Cradling the box in one arm, he opened the door and then shoved the cardboard container at his friend. "You're late. You're supposed to be helping me pack."

"You can't afford me," Trenton warned him. "Remember how much I charge an hour."

"I don't know," Chance said. "You have yet to show me a bill."

"I can show you some shrapnel scars instead. Those have marked your bill paid in full."

Chance waved off his friend's comments. They had talked freely about what had happened in Afghanistan, about the ambush that had injured Trenton. Chance, having escaped the roadside bomb without a scratch, had carried him to safety. "Old scars aren't getting you out of packing."

"I brought someone that might."

"You hired movers?"

"No, I brought Robyn." He lowered the box to the floor and stepped to the side, so that Chance could see around him to the woman standing on the porch. She seemed reluctant to come any closer. The puppy jumped around her legs now, trying to lick her hands, which Robyn held out as if to ward off the animal.

Chance's stomach pitched with nerves at the sight of her. "Don't tell me you've changed your mind about the joint custody."

"I haven't changed my mind about that," she assured him. "Matthew wants you in his life."

Trenton ducked out of the house and around Robyn, then headed toward the porch steps, as if trying to sneak away. But Chance was as nervous about being alone with his ex as he was about her reasons for being there—despite her assurances.

"You're leaving?" Chance asked Trenton.

His friend nodded in reply. "You two don't need lawyers anymore."

"No," Chance agreed. "But I need a friend." Never more so than now, after having made the second toughest decision of his life.

"You need more than a friend," Trenton said. "You're just too stubborn and self-sacrificing to admit that." With a glance at Robyn, he headed down the steps and crossed the driveway to his sports car.

"He's right," she said, her voice just above a whisper. Then she smiled. "But don't you dare tell him I ever admitted that."

Trenton's flashy red car pulled out of the drive, and only the police car Chance had yet to turn back over to the sheriff's office remained. "You rode up here with him?" he asked.

She laughed. "Yeah, amazing we both made it alive."

Chance figured she'd always blamed Trenton for his staying in the reserves. It had been his friend's idea, when college loans had started mounting, to enlist. To help pay for Robyn's med school bills, Chance had signed up, too.

"Why are you here?" he asked. "I don't understand…" But he held open the door for her to enter, the dog still jumping around her legs. Once inside, Cookie scampered off to her food and water bowls in the kitchen, and Robyn followed, glancing around the house with interest.

"I didn't understand either until Trenton passed this on to me." She pulled a thin plastic chip from her pocket and held it out for him.

"What's he done now?" he murmured. His laptop lay open on the kitchen table, so he connected the memory card to a port and images began to play…of that first night he had felt he had a real family, when Jessie and Tommy had come over with dinner for him and Matthew and spent the night. She'd taken photos and video of him and the boys. Then there were the pictures from the park and, at the end, the audio of a conversation she'd had with Trenton.

No wonder his friend had left.

"How the hell did Trenton get this?" he asked, staring at the images flickering across the screen. Tommy liked to wield the camera, too, so there were pictures of Chance and Jessie together, staring at each other as if unable to look away. And there were Jessie and Matthew, her arm around the boy's shoulders, his around her waist with easy familiarity and affection.

"Jessie gave it to him last time he was here." She lifted a dark brow. "Turns out she's not a young boy."

"No, she's not," Chance said as an image of the beautiful redhead appeared on his laptop. "She really gave this to him?"

"Yeah. I think on a whim, or maybe because Trenton goaded her. He's good at that." Robyn shrugged. "When I called her about it, she apologized profusely. She'd had no idea her conversation with Trenton had been recorded."

"And you believe her?" he asked his cynical ex.

She lifted that brow again. "You don't?"

"I'm certain she had no idea," Chance said, firmly defending the woman he loved, "but I still don't understand why she gave it to Trenton to give to you."

"I do," Robyn said with a faint smile. "She's in love with you."

Chance's breath caught with hope. But then he pushed it aside because there was no possibility of living out that dream Jessie had recorded on her memory card. That was all it had been: a dream, not reality. "She didn't tell you that."

"She didn't have to," Robyn said, gesturing toward the computer screen. "I saw it. I heard it. There's no doubt that woman loves you. And that you're in love with her, too."

He could deny Jessie's feelings but not his own. All he could do was uphold the decision they'd already made. "It doesn't matter what we feel for each other."

"Since when doesn't love matter?" Robyn asked, her dark eyes wistful as if she had feelings of her own for someone she couldn't have.

It wasn't him. Chance had no doubt about that. Even before she'd filed for divorce, he'd known she hadn't loved him anymore—not like she once had.

"Love doesn't matter," he said, "when we're both determined to do what's best for our boys."

She pointed to the computer screen and the image of Matthew and Tommy playfully wrestling with the hyper puppy. "What if being together is what's best for the boys?"

"That's why I gave up my job," he reminded her, "so that I can be with my son. That's why I'm moving back to Chicago." He hadn't found a place of his own yet, but he could crash at Trenton's until he did.

"You hate the city," she said. "You always hated the city, but even more after you came back from Afghanistan. It'll kill you to live there."

"It'll kill me to be apart from my son any longer." He couldn't say goodbye to the boy again; being away from him had left Chance with a gaping hole in his heart.

"He hates the city, too," she acknowledged with a

sigh. "It didn't matter that I kept you two apart. He's still you—through and through." She blinked back tears of regret.

But Chance didn't believe she regretted that their son was like him but that she'd kept them apart. "I shouldn't have signed up," he admitted. "I shouldn't have left... either of you. I'm sorry."

"No. I was being selfish and spiteful. You were meant to go over there. If you hadn't, Trenton wouldn't have come back alive. Neither would so many others."

"But I didn't get back to that boy in time..." He'd broken that promise, the one he'd made to help the sick child whose family had had no access to medical assistance.

"I wish you would have told me about him." She shook her head, as if trying to shake off all her old resentments. "But we weren't exactly talking then."

"No."

"I think I was just looking for excuses," she said, "a reason to blame you for us going wrong when it was really me. I just didn't love you anymore."

"I know."

She nodded. "I don't think I ever loved you like Jessie Phillips does. She loves you enough to let you go—not hold you back from doing what you want to do."

He glanced around at the open boxes that he'd been struggling to pack. The only things he'd managed to put inside the cardboard cartons were items he'd inherited from his grandmother. The stuff that he and Jessie and Tommy had bought for the house or for Matthew—he couldn't toss them inside a box and close the lid. They were things he couldn't easily pack away.

"But this isn't what you want," she said, gesturing at

the boxes. "You don't want to move back to Chicago. You want to stay here."

"Are you trying to talk me into giving up my son?" Was that the purpose of this cryptic visit? Robyn had changed her mind about sharing custody.

She shook her head, her eyes filling with tears. "No. I'm trying to talk you into giving him more."

"Robyn?" He had never really understood this woman despite having been married to her. "I still don't know what you're telling me."

She sniffled as the tears streaked down her face. "What if the boys are best for each other?"

"What do you mean?"

"That little redheaded boy calls Matthew." She pointed at Tommy on the computer screen and smiled as if unable to help herself. "Of course on the phone he sounds like he's about forty. Not his voice, but his... wisdom."

"You talked to him too?"

She nodded. "I didn't call to interrogate him like I did his mother. I just answered Matthew's cell. I'd taken it away from him for throwing a fit about you and this place. But once I answered it, I spoke with Tommy for quite a while."

Chance laughed. "Yeah, forty sounds about right. Maybe sixty. The kid is..." *Precocious* didn't cover Tommy Phillips. "...amazing."

"She's done such a good job with him," Robyn said.

Chance nodded, impressed all over again with the way Jessie had managed alone. But then, in Forest Glen, no one was ever really alone. That was what he would miss most about the town. No. What he'd miss most was what he could have had…with Jessie and Tommy.

"She told me that I did a good job with Matthew," Robyn said, but she sounded skeptical.

"You have done a great job with our son," Chance assured her.

Tears shimmered on her lashes again. "No. I did a very bad thing when I kept him away from you, when I put my resentment and my career before Matthew's needs."

"What are you saying?"

"He needs to be here. With you." She gestured toward the computer monitor. "With them."

Chance gazed wistfully at the screen. It had stopped on a picture they'd taken with the timer on the camera. All of them were crowded together on the couch in the family room—everyone smiling and laughing as Cookie tried to lick Chance's face. "I appreciate what you're saying, but it's too late."

"It should never be too late for love."

It didn't matter that he had finally come to his senses. Jessie wanted what was best for her son, too, and that meant a relationship with his real father. For both Tommy and her.

JESSIE HAD NEVER BEEN so miserable—not even when she'd been pregnant and alone and forced to move to a small town and live with relatives she hadn't known very well. Chance was moving today. Earlier, she'd seen the rental truck drive past the doctor's office on its way to his house. No one else was leaving Forest Glen; it had to be *his* truck.

Overwhelmed with the sense of loss, she stepped onto the porch. But still she couldn't breathe, not even with the warm summer breeze swirling around the house. She couldn't think about anything but Chance leaving. For good.

The door creaked open behind her, and she turned to see Keith let himself out. Despite renting a place right in town, he spent a lot of time here. With Tommy. And with her.

"Are you feeling okay?" he asked. His eyes—the eyes Tommy had inherited—were as warm as the breeze with concern. And something else, something Jessie couldn't reciprocate.

She nodded. "I'm fine."

Keith's mouth curved into a slight smile. "You've never been a very good liar, Jess."

"I guess not," she agreed. "You really knew that I was pregnant even though I told you I wasn't?"

"I didn't admit it to myself," he said. "I took you at your word because I wanted to. I was a coward who didn't want to face up to that kind of responsibility. I didn't want to grow up." He stepped closer and took her hand in his. "And because of that, you had to grow up too fast. You became a single mom when you were just a kid."

"I don't regret that—I don't regret having Tommy," she assured him. "I love him so much that every sacrifice I've had to make was worth it." Even letting Chance go without a fight.

"You shouldn't have had to sacrifice anything," Keith said, his thumb stroking over her knuckles. "I should have been with you, supporting you." His throat moved as he swallowed. "Loving you."

"I should have told you the truth. I shouldn't have denied you all these years with your son."

"You can make it up to me now," he said with a teasing grin. "And you can let me make it up to you for not being there when you needed me."

Her stomach churned with the realization that he was about to propose. Dreading it, she shook her head. "Keith…"

"I want to marry you," he said. "I want you and me to make a home for our son together. I want us to make a family for Tommy."

Tears of regret burned Jessie's eyes. Eight years ago, she'd wanted nothing more than for him to track her down and declare his undying love and devotion. That had been her dream for years. But now reality had set in, and her heart belonged to another man. "Keith, I wish I could say yes…"

But she wasn't as selfless as Chance. She couldn't give up everything to make Tommy happy—not when it would make her miserable. And being married to a man she didn't love would do that.

"But you can't say yes to me," he said with a sad smile of acceptance, as if he'd already known what her answer would be but felt he'd still had to ask. "I missed my chance eight years ago."

She shook her head. "It would have been a mistake back then, too. Your parents were right. We were too young to be as serious as we were."

He sighed. "Ah, young love. Does anything ever match its intensity?"

She didn't want to hurt him, but she nodded in reply. She knew now that what she'd had with Keith wasn't true love, the kind that lasted forever. The kind she felt for Chance would.

WITH HIS HAND SHAKING as if he were putting a worm on a hook, Tommy dropped his pencil. Then he lifted the piece of paper from the hardwood floor where, all hunched over, he'd been writing. He needed a desk, like the one built into the space between the windows in Matt's bedroom at Chance's house.

But he wasn't worried about furniture right now. He was worried about his note. He read it over again:

Mom, I'm sick of you and everybody else thinking I'm too young to understand stuff. I get it. I know what's best for me. I wish you did. But because you don't, I'm running away. You can look for me, but I won't come home till you stop treating me like a stupid baby. I'm not stupid.

He winced like he had a tooth hurting from a cavity. Was his note too mean?

He glanced at the phone, thinking about calling for help. But he'd promised he could handle this, that he wasn't too much of a baby to write a note. Mrs. Morris, his teacher, had said he had the best writing of everybody in the third grade class.

She'd told his mom that Tommy should probably just skip fourth grade so that he would be challenged next year. She hadn't known about the challenge he'd have this summer. He sighed and turned back to the note.

I love you, but I can't live here anymore. Your son, Tommy.

He snorted. Now that was stupid. She knew he was her son. But he didn't have time to fix it now, so he scrambled to his feet and carried the note to his bed and laid it on his pillow. He was supposed to be getting ready for bed, but instead he had his clothes on. His pajamas were in the backpack he grabbed up now from the floor.

He'd wanted to go out the window, but that part of the plan had been shot down. So he kept his word and snuck down the hall past Mom's bedroom. She sat on her bed, her back to him, and he could hear her sniffling like she had a cold. Or was crying.

A pang hit his heart like a dodge ball in the stomach. He wanted to crawl into bed with her and hug her until she stopped crying. But because he loved his mom, he couldn't. So he kept tiptoeing along the hall and then hurried down the stairs and through the house to the back door.

Because he loved his mom, he had to make her happy another way—a way that would last. Forever.

Chapter Sixteen

A fist hammered at Chance's door. After drawing in a breath to brace himself, he pulled it open to find Jessie. She rushed inside, her breathing heavy, as if she'd run over to his house. But her SUV was parked in the driveway behind his police car.

"I'm sorry to bother you," she said. "I know you're probably busy packing. But I need you—I need your help."

He grabbed her arms, trying to still her trembling. "I'm here for you. I'll *always* be here for you."

Her gaze clung to his, as if she were trying to figure out what he meant, what he'd just promised her. But then she shook her head, unwilling to be distracted. "Tommy's run away again!"

"He has?" His heart constricted at the worry that had washed the color from her beautiful face.

"I looked everywhere for him," she said. "He's not at Belinda's or the Johnsons' or even with Keith."

"No?" He fought the urge to tell her the truth, to spare her even another second of worry, but Chance had promised to stick to the plan. "Do you have any idea where else he might be?"

She drew in a shuddery breath and nodded. "I think he's probably in the tree house."

"We can check," he offered, shutting the front door behind her before following her down the hall to the kitchen.

She glanced at the open boxes on the floor. "It almost looks like you're unpacking now," she observed. "And the truck's gone."

"Truck?"

"Moving truck," she replied. "You sent it on without the rest of your stuff?"

Before he could think of an answer that wasn't an outright lie, she'd reached the back door. Her hand trembled on the knob as she twisted it. "I see lights." She exhaled a breath of relief. "He's here…"

She didn't pull the door open and rush into the yard, though. She just stared through the window at those flickering lights. "I—I don't know what to say to him," she admitted. "I don't know how to convince him to come home with me."

"Follow your heart," he suggested. But maybe, like him, she didn't think that was possible.

She turned back to him, scrutinizing his face. Despite her concern for her son, she must have picked up on the fact that Chance was trying to tell her something. "What do you mean?"

"You'll know," he assured her. "Once you get up there, you'll know." And hopefully she would take his advice and let her heart lead her where his had led him. To Forest Glen. And her.

JESSIE WASN'T AFRAID of heights, but she felt dizzy as she glanced down at Chance standing below the ladder she climbed. She'd been in the tree house before, praising the work as Tommy and Chance had built the structure her brilliant little boy had designed. She'd also brought up the boys' snacks, when Matthew had visited, and he and Tommy had tried to move into the little wooden house suspended above the backyard.

Even though she'd checked all those other places for Tommy first, she'd known this was where he'd gone. The minute she'd found that note on his pillow, when she'd come to tuck him into bed, she'd known he'd go to Chance. He and Keith had finally bonded, despite her son's resistance, but Chance was the man he turned to when he needed a shoulder to lean on. It was where his heart led him.

Like hers had led her here—to Chance. But she'd resisted following her heart, had resisted coming here, because she worried that she would break down and beg him to stay in Forest Glen, with her. And she loved him too much to make him choose between his son and her.

Despite what he'd written, Tommy didn't understand that what was best for him and her was not best for Chance. She braced herself to explain to him what she'd wished he would never have to learn—that sometimes there was no happy ending.

But as she climbed through the trapdoor in the floor, she released that breath in a gasp of disbelief. Candles flickered in glass jars placed in the corners of the little structure. Sleeping bags, strewn with rose petals, covered the floor. And beside the sleeping bags, beads of condensation trickled down the sides of a metal bucket holding a champagne bottle and ice.

But she was the only person in the place until Chance

climbed the ladder and joined her, kneeling on the sleeping bag next to her.

"What is all of this?" she asked, totally confused. She had no idea what was going on. Her son's note, Chance's weird comments... "Where's Tommy?"

"He's with Matthew."

She glanced toward the house, but the only light she glimpsed through the windows was in the kitchen. "Your son is here? They're both inside?" She doubted they'd be sleeping if they were together.

"They're not here," he said.

"Then where...?"

"They're with Robyn."

Heat rushed to her face as she remembered that uncomfortable phone conversation with his ex. Had the doctor told him how Jessie had interfered? Somehow she doubted that he would have set up the candles and champagne if he knew what she'd done. She shouldn't have given Trenton that memory card to give to Robyn, especially since she hadn't remembered everything on it.

"Tommy hasn't been gone long enough to make it to Chicago," she calculated. "Is Robyn here?"

He nodded. "She's rented a place in town for now." He grinned. "She was surprised she found it so easily. Finding an apartment in the city is like setting off on a quest for hidden treasure."

"People tend to move away from small towns," she said. "Not to them. Is she actually going to live here?" Jessie had suggested it during that long awkward phone conversation, but Robyn had only laughed.

"Yeah." A grin lit up his handsome face. "She's already packed up all of her and Matthew's stuff and had it moved here."

That must have been the truck she'd seen. It had been bringing someone to Forest Glen. Not taking him away. "So you're staying?"

He nodded.

"What about your job? You gave it up." And Chance wasn't the kind of guy who could *not* work.

"My replacement backed out. He changed his mind about living in a small town."

"And the mayor gave you the job back?"

"After a little persuasion," he said with a smile. "Like you persuaded Robyn."

Jessie smiled, too, although her heart was conflicted. She was glad Chance was happy, but she was also jealous of the joy he felt that his ex was moving to Forest Glen. "I still can't believe Matthew's mother is making that sacrifice."

When she'd talked to Robyn, she'd had no doubt that the woman loved her son very much. But she had a career and a life she'd worked hard to build. Had she given that up for Matthew? Or for Chance?

"She decided it was her turn to put Matthew first," he said, respect in his voice. "But she's also looking forward to a less hectic schedule than at the hospital. She's a general practitioner and has already talked to Dr. Malewitz about taking over his practice."

"He and Ruth told me they were looking for someone to do that." She had even mentioned it to Robyn, but she hadn't considered the consequences. "She'll be my boss, if she decides to keep me on."

"She likes you," he assured her. "She wants to meet you in person."

"She does?"

"Yes. But let's not talk about her or Keith or even the kids."

Hope flickered like the flames of those candles. He had gone to so much trouble to turn the boys' clubhouse into a romantic love nest. He had to have a reason. Dare she hope...

She swallowed hard, fighting down her nerves. "Then what should we talk about?"

"The future," he replied, his eyes bright with his own hope. "Our future. Together."

"Do we have one?" she asked.

"That's for you to decide," he said. "I'm on my knees, Jessie."

She fought a smile as she pointed out, "That's because the roof's not high enough for you to stand."

He shook his head and pulled a small velvet case from the pocket of his jeans. "No. I'm on my knees because I'm proposing."

"Why are you proposing?" she asked. "Because of the boys? Because they want to be a family?"

"They'll be happy as hell, and it's definitely what's best for them. But no." He grinned. "I'm asking you to be my wife because I'm selfish."

She couldn't fight the smile anymore. "You are?"

"Yes, I want to spend the rest of my life with the woman I love."

"So you don't care what anyone else wants?" she teased.

"I do," he said. "I care about what you want. What do you want, Jessie?"

She rose to her knees beside him and looped her arms around his neck. "You. I want you."

He kissed her, brushing his lips gently across hers as if he needed to control his desire for her. He pulled back. "Why do you want me, Jessie?"

"Because I love you." Tears blurred her vision, and she blinked them away so she could focus on his face, see how his happiness made him more handsome than ever.

"So will you marry me?" he asked. "Will you spend the rest of your life with me?"

"Yes!" she shouted her response. And she kissed him, letting all her love pour from her lips to his as her fingers clenched his soft hair.

With a groan, he pulled his mouth from hers and removed her hands from his hair. "We need to make this official," he said. "People will want proof that we've finally stopped acting like idiots."

"People?" she asked, a smile tugging at her lips.

"Our sons."

Our sons. Tears threatened again, but she didn't want to miss a minute of Chance's proposal. She wanted to commit every detail to memory—to share with their children and, someday, their grandchildren.

He flipped open the jewelry box, and her breath caught with surprise at the size and shape of the glittering diamond. "Matt and Tommy helped me pick it out," he said. "I hope you like it."

She couldn't stop the tears now as they flowed freely down her face. "I love it!" She held out her trembling hand, and he slid the heart-shaped solitaire onto her finger. "Follow your heart," she murmured.

"And take mine," he said. "I love you so much. And I will spend the rest of my life giving you everything you want."

She wrapped her arms around his neck again, clinging to him. "I have everything I want right now."

"Right now?" he asked.

She nodded. "In the future I'm going to want more kids. Hopefully a little sister for our boys."

"I think I can manage that. We'll just keep trying until we have her."

She smiled. "Why do I have a feeling I'm going to wind up living in a house filled with testosterone?"

"You're going to wind up living in a house full of love," he assured her. "Will it be this house?"

"Oh, yeah," she replied. "This house is home." And this man was the one she was meant to share that house with. But not just yet. "Can we spend the night here," she asked, "in the tree house?"

"That's the plan."

"So Tommy's note—" it had nearly given her a stroke "—it was part of the plan?"

"I'm sorry." He apologized with a kiss at her temple. Then his lips skimmed along her cheek to the corner of her mouth. "I didn't want to hurt you, but I needed to get you to come to me."

"And I needed to realize that what's best for Tommy is doing what's best for me." She glanced down at the ring again. "Following my heart...right to you..."

He kissed her again. But kissing wasn't enough. His hands tugged up her T-shirt and pulled it over her head. Her hair spilled around her bare shoulders. The thin shirt and boxer shorts were the clothes she wore to bed—all she wore to bed. She hadn't bothered changing when she'd found Tommy's note so she didn't have a bra on. Only her hair covered her naked breasts. But Chance's hands, shaking slightly, pushed back the red locks. Then his palms covered her breasts, stroking over the sensitive points, so that she arched into him.

He groaned, then lowered his head and kissed her breasts as thoroughly and passionately as he'd kissed her mouth. His tongue stroked over her nipple, teasing, until the pressure wound so tightly inside her she nearly came from his exquisite torture.

But he'd already been the selfless one. So she pushed him back onto the makeshift bed of sleeping bags and rose petals, and she dragged off his shirt and unsnapped his jeans. He lifted his hips and shucked off the denim and the briefs beneath them. Then she leaned over him, teasing him first with her hair and then with her lips— skimming both across the hard, hair-dusted muscles of his broad chest and over his rippling abs. She dipped her tongue in his navel before trailing it down the length of his erection.

He groaned and fisted his hands in her hair. He urged her back up his body until her mouth met his. Then he kissed her deeply, his tongue sliding between her lips and over her tongue. His hands traveled down her naked back to her hips, and he pushed off the boxers. Then he made love to her with his mouth, kissing her intimately as she writhed beneath him until finally the pressure broke free.

She screamed his name as she came. Then she lifted her legs and wrapped them around his waist as he thrust inside her. In perfect harmony, their bodies mated while their hearts and souls bonded. They'd only become engaged, but it felt as though they were already married. As one, they catapulted into ecstasy.

Clasped in each other's arms, they didn't stir until the

candles burned low. Only a faint glow painted shadows across the tree house and Chance's hard muscles.

"I understand now," she murmured happily.

"What?" he asked as he stroked his hands over her bare skin, making her tingle with awareness and pleasure.

"I get what you and the boys see in this place." She never wanted to leave it or Chance's arms. "Think we can honeymoon here?"

"We can honeymoon wherever you want," he said. "I'm going to spend the rest of my life making you happy."

She believed him. Because Chance Drayton kept his promises.

Epilogue

As Thomas "Tommy" Phillips crossed the stage to accept his diploma, he glanced out at the crowd screaming his name. Eight years ago, when it had been pretty much just him and his mom, he'd never imagined that one day he would have a family this big.

He had only asked Sheriff Chance Drayton to find his dad. The man had kept his promise and then some. Chance had given him—and his mom—so much more.

His blood brother cheered from the other side of the stage since Matt had already accepted his diploma. Like that third grade teacher had recommended, Thomas had skipped fourth grade and then sixth and had caught up with his "big" brother. Not only were they graduating together but they were heading off to the same college in the fall. Thomas for pre-med, Matt for pre-law.

Robyn whistled from the audience. She was thrilled that he was following in her footsteps and was already planning on sharing her practice with him. And Matt was following in his stepdad's footsteps. Like Trenton Sanders, he planned to first get his law degree and then enter politics. The mayor now, Trenton had a seat behind the podium since he'd given the keynote address before turning over the mike for Thomas to give his speech as valedictorian.

Thomas had talked about the importance of family—about their unwavering love and support. He'd also promised that if you believed in your dreams, you could make them come true, like he had. His family had cheered the loudest then, his little sister waving her arms wildly from her perch on his dad's shoulders. But Jennifer wasn't just his sister; she was also his cousin since his dad had married his mom's cousin Belinda.

His family wasn't just big but convoluted as hell. Thomas didn't care. He loved it—and all of them. But nobody as much as his mom. She was raising his younger brothers with the same love and devotion she'd given him. He'd be sharing that practice with Robyn and his mom, since she'd been the RN on staff for the past seven years.

After shaking the principal's hand, he lifted the diploma in his fist, holding it up for all the clicking cameras. He crossed his eyes over his nose and sucked in his cheeks for his signature fish face, which had Matt laughing as hard as he had when they'd first met. Then, photo op over, he found his mom in the crowd, on her feet despite being so pregnant she could barely fit through the narrow aisle between the chairs the school had set up in the park.

He rushed through the crowd and threw his arms around her—as far as they could reach. And over her head, he met Chance's proud gaze. And he mouthed, "Thank you…"

* * * * *

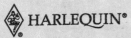

HARLEQUIN®

COMING NEXT MONTH

Available October 12, 2010

#1325 THE TRIPLETS' FIRST THANKSGIVING
Babies & Bachelors USA
Cathy Gillen Thacker

#1326 ELLY: COWGIRL BRIDE
The Codys: The First Family of Rodeo
Trish Milburn

#1327 THE RELUCTANT WRANGLER
Roxann Delaney

#1328 FAMILY MATTERS
Barbara White Daille

HARCNM0910

REQUEST YOUR FREE BOOKS!
2 FREE NOVELS PLUS 2 FREE GIFTS!

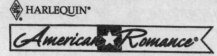

Love, Home & Happiness!

HARLEQUIN®

A Romance

FOR EVERY MOOD™

Spotlight on

Inspirational

Wholesome romances
that touch the heart and soul.

See the next page
to enjoy a sneak peek from
the Love Inspired® inspirational series.

*See below for a sneak peek at
our inspirational line, Love Inspired®.
Introducing HIS HOLIDAY BRIDE
by bestselling author Jillian Hart*

Autumn Granger gave her horse rein to slide toward the town's new sheriff.

"Hey, there." The man in a brand-new Stetson, black T-shirt, jeans and riding boots held up a hand in greeting. He stepped away from his four-wheel drive with "Sheriff" in black on the doors and waded through the grasses. "I'm new around here."

"I'm Autumn Granger."

"Nice to meet you, Miss Granger. I'm Ford Sherman, from Chicago." He knuckled back his hat, revealing the most handsome face she'd ever seen. Big blue eyes contrasted with his sun-tanned complexion.

"I'm guessing you haven't seen much open land. Out here, you've got to keep an eye on cows or they're going to tear your vehicle apart."

"What?" He whipped around. Sure enough, mammoth black-and-white creatures had started to gnaw on his four-wheel drive. They clustered like a mob, mouths and tongues and teeth bent on destruction. One cow tried to pry the wiper off the windshield, another chewed on the side mirror. Several leaned through the open window, licking the seats.

"Move along, little dogie." He didn't know the first thing about cattle.

The entire herd swiveled their heads to study him curiously. Not a single hoof shifted. The animals soon returned to chewing, licking, digging through his possessions.

Autumn laughed, a warm and wonderful sound. "Thanks,

I needed that." She then pulled a bag from behind her saddle and waved it at the cows. "Look what I have, guys. Cookies."

Cows swung in her direction, and dozens of liquid brown eyes brightened with cookie hopes. As she circled the car, the cattle bounded after her. The earth shook with the force of their powerful hooves.

"Next time, you're on your own, city boy." She tipped her hat. The cowgirl stayed on his mind, the sweetest thing he had ever seen.

Will Ford be able to stick it out in the country to find out more about Autumn? Find out in HIS HOLIDAY BRIDE by bestselling author Jillian Hart, available in October 2010 only from Love Inspired®.

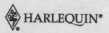